MANTIS

K19 SECURITY SOLUTIONS

BOOK FOUR

HEATHER SLADE

MANTIS

© 2018 Heather Slade

Paperback:
ISBN 13: 978-1-942200-62-8

MORE FROM AUTHOR HEATHER SLADE

BUTLER RANCH
Prequel: *Kade's Worth*
Book One: *Brodie*
Book Two: *Maddox*
Book Three: *Naughton*
Book Four: *Mercer*
Book Five: *Kade*

K19 SECURITY SOLUTIONS
Book One: *Razor*
Book Two: *Gunner*
Book Three: *Mistletoe*
Book Four: *Mantis*
Book Five: *Dutch*
Book Six: *Striker*
Book Seven: *Monk*
Book Eight: *Halo*
Book Nine: *Tackle*
Coming soon:
Book Ten: *Onyx*

MILITARY INTELLIGENCE
SECTION 6
Book One: *Shiver*
Book Two: *Wilder*
Book Three: *Pinch*
Book Four: *Shadow*

THE INVINCIBLES
Book One: *Decked*
Book Two: *Edged*
Book Three: *Grinded*
Book Four: *Riled*
Book Five: *Smoked*
Book Six: *Bucked*
Book Seven: *Irished*
Coming soon:
Book Eight: *Sainted*

ROARING FORK RANCH
Coming soon:
Book One: *Roughstock*
Book Two: *Rockstar*

COWBOYS OF
CRESTED BUTTE
Book One: *Fall for Me*
Book Two: *Dance with Me*
Book Three: *Kiss Me Cowboy*
Book Four: *Stay with Me*
Book Five: *Win Me Over*

COCKY HERO CLUB
Undercover Agent

KB WORLDS
EVERYDAY HEROES:
Handled

TABLE OF CONTENTS

Chapter 1 1

Chapter 2 3

Chapter 3 6

Chapter 4 14

Chapter 5 16

Chapter 6 19

Chapter 7 33

Chapter 8 36

Chapter 9 42

Chapter 10 46

Chapter 11 48

Chapter 12 53

Chapter 13 63

Chapter 14 65

Chapter 15 69

Chapter 16 72

Chapter 17 76

Chapter 18 78

Chapter 19 83

Chapter 20 86

Chapter 21 90

Chapter 22 93

Chapter 23 95

1

Dutch

When I donned my night-vision device, I could see my target along with two other men, who looked like they were also prisoners. All were heavily guarded by a band of Somali pirates.

This was K19 Security Solution's second extraction in the same number of weeks. The team had initially been summoned to Somalia to aid in a CIA rescue of two operatives who had been captives of a different band of pirates. Those two men—along with the majority of K19's team—had gotten out safely and were back stateside, enjoying what was left of the Christmas holiday.

My target, Gehring "Mantis" Cassman, hadn't been as fortunate. On his way back to Mogadishu, he was intercepted and taken hostage by the rangy group of thugs standing guard over him now.

Unlike with the majority of our extractions, the group holding Mantis and the other two men was unorganized, financially crippled, and in seemingly poor health themselves.

That wasn't unusual in Somalia, where over one million people were displaced, half of those in Mogadishu alone. The vast majority of the small nation's citizens relied heavily on assistance just to survive.

Given the Somali jihadist fundamentalist groups with ties to al-Qaeda frequently intercepted any aid that came into the country, financial or otherwise, thousands of people died daily.

Gangs of pirates, like the ones my team and I were about to take out, routinely kidnapped whomever they could get their hands on with the hope that they'd win the "black market lottery" of a paid ransom.

Like the odds of winning an actual lottery, most of the time, those kidnapped had little or no money, or in Mantis' case, a government that refused to negotiate with terrorists.

I wasn't here to negotiate. I was here to extract.

"In on three," I said to my teammates, Ranger and Diesel, through the mic on my headset.

"Roger that," both CIA operatives responded.

My count commenced, and within seconds, the encampment was bombarded with a hail of bullets, as my team and I systematically took out the Somalis.

2

Mantis

When I heard the sound that made my ears prick up, I knew all hell would soon rain down on the encampment where I was being held hostage. The nausea and debilitating headache I'd had only moments ago went away with the rush of adrenaline that flooded my body. Every nerve ending had gone on high alert as I prepared to carry out the procedures I'd been trained to do if I ever found myself in a hostage situation.

My job was to get myself and the other two captives out of the way without alerting our Somali pirate captors of the impending attack.

As with every other mission or op I'd carried out with my lifelong best friend, Thomas "Dutch" Miller, it executed flawlessly.

"Let's go!" Dutch shouted, leading me and the other hostages out of the compound and into waiting vehicles.

I climbed into one SUV with Dutch, and the other four men climbed into the second.

"I owe ya one," I said once we were a safe distance away from the compound.

Dutch laughed. "Oh, yeah? I think I owed you a couple first."

"Let's call it even, then. What's the word on Striker, Tackle, and Halo?"

"Extracted." Dutch scrubbed his face with his hand. "I'm not sure if I should tell you this."

I turned my head and looked at him. "What?"

"They were home in time for Christmas."

I nodded. That wasn't bad news. I wondered why Dutch would think I'd take it as such.

"How are you doin'?"

I rubbed the back of my neck with my hand. "I could use a hot shower, about five gallons of water, and decent food. After that—sleep."

"Tall order, but I think we can manage most of it. Who were the other two prisoners?"

"I don't know. They're not American, I know that much."

"Diesel and Ranger will take care of contacting whichever embassy they should be delivered to."

"How far are we from Mogadishu?"

"Three hours, at least."

"Mind if I get some rest?"

"Of course not."

I reached over the back of the seat and grabbed a blanket. I wadded it up and put it between my head and the passenger side window. As uncomfortable as I was, it was better than where I'd been sleeping the last several days.

3

Alegria

"Anything?" I asked Onyx, K19 Security Solutions'
handler for the mission to extract Mantis.

"Negative, ma'am," he reported.

I paced the living room of the small guest house
where I'd been staying since right before Christmas,
and closed my eyes, wishing Dutch and I had been able
to clear the air before he left. Things hadn't been right
between us since before Thanksgiving.

After a bullet hit me in the back, causing damage to
my spinal cord, I'd undergone emergency surgery. When
I first came to, Dutch hadn't been the man sitting at my
hospital bedside. Instead, Mantis was.

At first, I thought I must be dreaming, seeing the
man who had been the love of my life for as long as I
could remember there next to me. But then I'd looked
across the room to see Dutch was there too. Not knowing what else to do, I'd reached out to him.

In that instant, it had become clear that Mantis had
no idea Dutch and I were together.

* * *

"That wasn't fair, Alegria," Dutch scolded me after Mantis stormed out of the room without a word. "You made him think—"

"That I'd moved on."

"With me."

I caressed the back of his hand with my thumb. "Haven't I?"

"If I believed it's what you really want..."

"It is what I want."

Dutch scrubbed his face with his hand. "I know you still love him."

There was no point in lying; I would always love Mantis, but that didn't mean we could be together again. Both of us had said too many things we couldn't take back. I'd given him an ultimatum, and he'd chosen the mission over me.

That's just who Mantis was. From the day I'd met him at the United States Air Force Academy, he'd never wavered in his commitment to the military, and then to the CIA. I'd never been first with him, and I'd made it clear that if he wanted me in his life, he had to change his priorities. When he refused, I knew if I didn't end the relationship then, I never would. And I'd be miserable.

"I'm with you now. What I had with him is...over," I said to Dutch, who shook his head.

"I wish I could believe it was that simple."

"Why are you angry with me?"

He ran one hand through his hair while he grasped my fingers with the other. "Because I saw what just happened. Worse, I felt it."

"You didn't stop him from leaving. If you don't want to be with me, why didn't you tell him so?"

"I didn't say I don't want to be with you. As to why I didn't stop Mantis from leaving, I can't answer that. I guess it's because as much as I care about him, I care about you too, and right now, you need me more."

"I don't want your pity."

Dutch looked away. "What do you want?"

I bit my lip. "I...I don't know how to answer that."

He met my gaze. "Ask me."

"What?"

"Ask me what I want."

"What do you want, Dutch?" I whispered.

"I want to believe that someday you'll love me half as much as you love Mantis. Just half as much."

Dutch got up and walked out, but he'd come back, and when he did, I wasn't sure I'd be able to say anything that would convince him I could love him the way he wanted me to.

***

8

It wasn't much better after Dutch brought me home from the hospital. If we talked at all, it inevitably ended in an argument.

We were both irritable. For me, the frustration of my body healing and being limited in what I could do was compounded by the effects of withdrawal from the pain medication I'd decided to wean myself from. My doctor had disagreed and told me it was too soon, but I knew my own body. I'd been trained to withstand far worse pain. I wasn't just a pilot; I was a goddamn intelligence operative. There was no way I'd let something like this keep me down.

It was hard to believe it was only a few days ago that Dutch came to tell me he was leaving, and that now, he was God knew where, rescuing the man who hadn't just been my first love, but also Dutch's best friend.

* * *

Out of nowhere, a chill traveled up my spine, leaving me unable to shake the feeling of dread it left in its wake.

"Manon…we need to talk," Dutch said when I went to look for him and found him in the kitchen.

"About?"

"A mission…"

My eyes met his. "What is it?"

"Mantis. There's a report that he's been kidnapped by Somali pirates. I'm going in with a team to extract him."

"When do you leave?" I asked, knowing it had to be soon.

"Tonight. Look, I know it's close to Christmas, and I'm sorry—"

I held up my hand. "Don't be. I understand."

"I wasn't sure you would."

"What do you mean?"

"If Mantis had sprung something like this on you..."

I rested my hand on his arm. "This is different. If the situations were reversed and he was telling me he had to go in and get you, I would understand in the same way I do now."

Dutch reached out and stroked my cheek. "We'll leave at sixteen hundred."

I nodded and moved closer to him, wishing we hadn't spent the last three weeks arguing as much as we had. I wrapped my arms around his waist and rested my head on his chest.

When he leaned down and brought his lips to mine, I moved my hands from his waist to his butt, tilting my pelvis so his hardness was pressed against me.

"Are you sure you want this?" he murmured before he kissed me a second time.

I backed away, taking his hand and leading him into the bedroom.

I pulled my sweater over my head and then pushed my wool skirt down until it slid from my hips to the floor. Dutch's eyes traveled the length of my body; I stood before him in nothing but a bra and panties.

"Make love to me, Dutch." I held my hand out and sat on the bed.

In seconds he was on me, as though he was hurrying to get me naked before he changed his mind. His fingers released the clasp on my bra, and he pulled it from my body.

"Lie down," he said, taking my panties in both hands and sliding them down my legs.

"Please, Dutch," I begged as he stood above me, taking his time looking at every inch of my nakedness.

I watched him undress. When we'd first met, he'd been tall and lanky, but over the course of the years, the boyishness of his body matured. While he may appear less muscular than some of the other K19 partners, he was no less powerful.

When he was happy, his blue eyes twinkled, and when he was focused on something, like he was on me now, their intensity heated my core. Dutch had let his beard grow and while at first I didn't like the way it scratched my skin, as it softened, I'd learned to love it.

The muscles in his body flexed as he stalked to the bedside table. I couldn't wait for this man to be inside me. It had been too long since he had.

He pulled out a foil packet from the drawer, rolled on the condom, and came to rest between my legs. His eyes bored into mine. "Do you know how much I love you?"

I nodded, but couldn't look him in the eye.

"Alegria, look at me..."

I shook my head, looking everywhere but at him. Moments ago I'd wanted him so badly, but now, all I could see was the look on Mantis' face when he stormed out of the hospital room. "I'm sorry..."

Dutch got off the bed and went into the bathroom. He came back out seconds later, grabbed his clothes, and stalked from the bedroom.

"Get dressed. We'll leave as soon as you're ready."

* * *

Equally painful was the way Dutch and I had parted ways before he left for Somalia. There hadn't been enough time for me to tell him I was sorry, or to assure him that I did love him—even if it wasn't in the way he wanted me to.

He'd parked the car in the Annapolis driveway of his teammate's mother's house, where the K19 partners were gathering for the holiday, walked around the car and opened my door. When I'd walked toward the house, he didn't follow.

"Aren't you coming inside?"

"Just to bring your bag in."

I'd walked back to him and rested my hand on his heart, wishing things could be different. "Be safe," I'd murmured, brushing his lips with mine.

He grabbed the back of my neck, hard. "Is that for me or him?" The edge in his voice startled me.

I raised my chin. "For both of you."

"I love you so fucking much, Alegria."

As much as I'd wanted to say the words back to him, I wasn't able to.

**

Now, days later, all I wanted to do was hear his voice. Whether he told me he loved me or only that he was safe, didn't matter.

"Still nothing?" I asked Onyx, who shook his head.

I had a bad feeling about what should have been a routine extraction for the team Dutch led. Instead of hearing that the op was complete, we weren't hearing anything.

4

Dutch

Something wasn't right with Mantis. I'd felt the shift when he first got back from Afghanistan, but then all hell broke loose for the entire K19 team, and there was no time for anyone to think beyond the mission at hand.

That op had ended with Alegria getting shot and then the incident in the hospital between the three of us. After that, Mantis had closed himself off to me completely.

At first his anger made sense, but the more I thought about it, the more I realized there was something far worse wrong.

Beneath the bravado of Mantis being pissed about me and Alegria, sat an apathy that I'd never seen in him before. Since we met on In-Processing Day at the Air Force Academy, he'd had a fire in him like I'd never seen.

His drive to serve his country, to combat terrorism and other evil in the world, was unwavering. He was intransigently steadfast in what he believed was right and wrong. There had never been gray with Mantis; everything had always been black or white.

Thinking back on it, I hadn't seen anything remotely close to conviction in Mantis since he returned from an op that should've been the crowning achievement of his life's work.

Few knew or ever would that he'd singlehandedly taken out Bagish Safi. While many believed Dadvar Safi was the mastermind behind the 9-11 attacks on the World Trade Center and the Pentagon, most in the intelligence community agreed that Dadvar's brother Bagish was the one truly responsible for taking the idea to Osama bin Laden in the first place.

I knew an opportunity like this, being alone with Mantis for a three-hour drive, would never present itself again.

His kidnapping by the Somali pirates had left him vulnerable, which I knew I shouldn't exploit, but I had to. If I didn't try to get Mantis to talk to me now, he never would.

5

Mantis

I opened my eyes when I felt the SUV come to a stop. "What the fuck?" I asked Dutch, who was looking out the driver's side window at the same nothingness I had.

"We need to talk."

"No, we don't."

"We aren't going anywhere until you tell me where the hell the man I've known since we were eighteen years old disappeared to, cuz I'll tell you what, I don't know you at all."

"You're full of shit. Just because you—"

"This has nothing to do with me. What happened in Afghanistan?"

I scrubbed my face with my hand. "Nothing."

"Wrong answer. *Something happened.*"

"I hunted down the target, and I killed him. End of story."

"What about Alegria?"

"The woman you couldn't keep your fucking hands off? What about her, Dutch?"

"You want her back?"

"Fuck you."

"If you do, I'll make it happen."

I wasn't sure which I wanted to do more: get out of the SUV in the middle of the goddamn desert or kill Dutch with my bare hands. The way I saw it, those were my only two choices.

"If you want to try to make it work with her, I'll walk away."

"You think it's that simple? What is she, a thing to pass back and forth between us?" I shook my head. "And you say you love her."

I didn't want to fucking talk about Afghanistan, and I sure as hell didn't want to talk about Alegria. Particularly with the man she was currently sleeping with.

"Either you want her back or you don't. It isn't complicated."

"You're a bastard."

Dutch put the vehicle into gear and pulled away from the side of the road. "If you want her back, just say so. How hard can that be?"

Of course I did; she was the goddamn love of my life. No woman could ever mean as much to me as she did, but what I wanted didn't matter. When I came back from Afghanistan, the armpit of the fucking world, she'd wanted nothing to do with me.

"What happened between you two?"

It was none of Dutch's business, but I answered him anyway. "I can't be the man she needs me to be."

"According to who? You or her?"

"When I came back, I had every intention of telling her I wanted to try to make it work between us."

"And?"

"She said no."

"Wait. You had every intention of telling her means you didn't, so how could she say no?"

"She wasn't interested in talking to me."

"What happened?"

"She wasn't interested. End of story. You're with her. You should know this."

Dutch nodded but didn't say anything.

"You two *are* together, right?"

Dutch shrugged. "It's complicated. Her surgery... you. She says it's over, but I know she still loves you."

"I can't be who she needs."

"That's what she says."

"Then why did you ask? Why are you making this complicated? It doesn't sound like there's any problem other than the one you're creating."

"I love her enough to want her to be happy."

"Do what it takes to make her so."

6

Alegria

"They're on their way to Mogadishu," Onyx said, setting down his phone after another call with Doc.

"What's their ETA?"

"A little over two hours. Their signal is spotty. Dutch told Doc he'd check in again once they reached the city. That's all I know for now, ma'am."

"Thank God," I murmured. "Onyx, you don't have to call me ma'am. We're equal partners in K19."

He smiled and shook his head. "Habit. It's the same with Doc. He always says he isn't the boss, but even Gunner, Razor, and Mercer think of him that way."

What Onyx said was true. Kade "Doc" Butler was the sometimes-reluctant head of K19 Security Solutions even though there were three other founding partners— Tabon "Razor" Sharp, Gunner Godet, and Mercer "Eighty-eight" Bryant. Doc's wife, Merrigan, was the fifth to be considered a "senior" partner and was also the official managing director.

Besides Onyx and me, there were three other former operatives who had recently joined the firm as "junior" partners—Dutch, Griffin "Striker" Ellis, and Rhys "Monk" Perrin. I'd heard that an offer was extended to Mantis, but he hadn't accepted. I wondered if he'd declined because of my relationship with Dutch.

Every partner, whether junior or senior, had served in at least one branch of the military and had also worked for the CIA, where most of our contracted work came from. The K19 team specialized in black and clandestine ops, asset protection, interrogation, and when necessary—assassination. Thus, extracting one of our own from a hostage situation before their true identity became known was always paramount.

"You should get some rest, ma'am," said Onyx, once again using the unnecessary honorific.

I could probably do as he suggested now that I knew both of the men who had been part of my life since I was a teenager were safe.

I'd been fresh off a plane from France and about to enter the United States Air Force Academy as a French foreign exchange cadet when I'd met them.

At the time, I'd had every intention of returning to my home country after I graduated, but when the Air

Force offered me a pilot training slot, I knew I'd spend my life in the country that was willing to make my dreams of being a fighter pilot come true.

There had been another reason I didn't return to France—Gehring "Mantis" Cassman. For a long time, I believed we'd spend our lives together. We'd get married, have a family, leave the military, and maybe become commercial airline pilots.

The deeper we got into the covert activities of the CIA after we'd both retired from the Air Force, the less I believed that dream would ever come true. The separate missions we were assigned kept us apart for months at a time.

Our relationship suffered the most after we'd both returned from different six-month ops. I'd planned a vacation to France for us, but within days of being home, Mantis informed me that he was deploying again. I'd been as livid as I was disappointed, and when I'd told him so, we broke up for the first time in what would become many.

"It's never been a secret that I take my duty very seriously," he'd said.

"And I don't?"

"It isn't the same for you."

"What does that mean?" I'd had to prod him to continue, and finally, he suggested that because I hadn't been born in the United States, I couldn't possibly have the same level of commitment to service that he had. I'd slapped his face.

The roller-coaster ride of missing each other so much after being apart for weeks or months, getting back together, and then breaking up again, continued for years. Until one day, I'd had enough.

I'd never stopped loving him, though. Somewhere in the back of my mind, I hoped he'd realize I was more important to him than his duty, but so far, that hadn't happened. And even if it did, it was too late. I was with Dutch now.

"Ma'am," I heard Onyx say from the other side of the closed door.

"Coming."

"Sorry to wake you."

When he handed me the phone, I grabbed it. "Hello?"

"Hey, sweetheart," said Dutch.

"God, it's good to hear your voice. I've been so worried."

"Sorry I couldn't get in touch sooner. Things in Somalia are worse than we ever could have imagined."

"Where are you now?"

"On our way to B-Dog."

I was familiar with the former Soviet airstrip located about seventy miles north of Mogadishu. The US was dramatically expanding its military force in Somalia, and Baledogle Base was the unofficial headquarters for the teams of Special Forces operatives who were directing the nation's shadow war.

"How long will you be there?" I asked, hoping he would say they were shipping out right away.

"Not sure at this point. We have a briefing at zero seven hundred tomorrow."

I checked my watch. Eleven in the morning here meant it was eight in the evening in Mogadishu.

"How...are you?"

"I'm fine, but my guess is what you really want to ask is how Mantis is. Here, I'll put him on."

"Dutch? Wait..."

"Yeah?"

"What I really want to know is how you both are."

"Don't worry, Flygirl. It's all good."

I cringed. Flygirl was what Mantis had called me since we were both assigned to Laughlin Air Force Base in Texas for pilot training. He'd been a member of the squadron that gave me the call sign Alegria. Mantis called me that too, but when it was just the two of us, he either called me Manon or Flygirl.

I heard the phone shuffle and then the deep breath Mantis took before speaking.

"Hi," I said.

"Hey."

"Rough mission."

"Listen—"

"I didn't mean anything by that, Mantis. I heard it was rough, that's all."

"Right. Sorry. I'm pretty beat."

"I'm glad you're safe. Dutch too. Please tell him I'll talk to him later."

I disconnected the call before Mantis could say anything else. Feelings warred inside me. Hearing his voice set my blood on fire with longing to be in his arms. Two simple words, though, had hurled them right back into the fray of misunderstanding, accusations, and the inability to communicate.

I walked into the living room of the guest house to return Onyx's phone, but he wasn't there.

He'd probably gone back to the main house where some of the K19 partners were gathered with each other and their families.

The property where I was staying belonged to Gunner Godet's mother, who had graciously offered to host the team for the holidays. I doubted Madeline had anticipated that almost a week later, some of us would still be here.

"*Bon matin,*" Madeline said when I walked in the back door of the main house and into the kitchen.

I smiled. Gunner's grandfather on his mother's side had been the US Ambassador to France, and Madeline had spent most of her childhood living there.

"*Bon matin,*" I answered.

"I hear there's good news."

"Dutch and Mantis are on their way to the base north of Mogadishu."

"I'm so glad." Madeline walked over and hugged me. "I was on your side of too many missions in my life. When the call comes in and you know your loved ones are safe, it's as though the weight of the world is lifted off your shoulders."

Gunner's father, who had recently passed away, had retired as a four-star general from the United States Marine Corps. The missions he'd undertaken throughout the course of his career were as legendary as they were dangerous.

"What can I get you?" Madeline asked, opening the refrigerator.

I'd only had coffee this morning, and hadn't eaten much in the last couple of days. Suddenly, I was ravenous. "Whatever you have," I answered. "I can get it though."

"I don't mind. I love to cook." Madeline took eggs and bacon out of the refrigerator and set them on the counter. "Breakfast okay?"

"It's perfect, thank you." I dug the phone out of my back pocket. "I'll just return this to Onyx."

"He's in the living room. They're supposed to be taking down decorations, but I think they're spending more time playing with those puppies."

"That's right. The puppies." Three had been delivered as gifts on Christmas morning. One to Gunner and his fiancée, Zary; another to Ava, Razor's wife; and the final to Razor's sister, Saylor, and his nieces.

Saylor and the girls had left the day before, but Razor, Ava, Gunner, and Zary were all still here, which meant two of the puppies were too. My back hurt just thinking about the rambunctious animals.

"Sit," Madeline said, pulling out the chair. "I'll deliver this." She took the phone out of my hand and left the kitchen.

"Thank you," I said when she came back.

"You're welcome. How's your physical therapy going?"

I laughed. "I guess you caught the look on my face when I pictured playing with the *puppies*."

Madeline smiled and nodded.

"I need to start up again." I stood and stretched my back. The challenge to do so was that my original physical therapist was in California. I'd been seeing a different one at Langley after Thanksgiving when Dutch and I went to stay at his place in Newport News. It was a four-hour drive from here to there, and even if I attempted it, with Dutch still in Somalia, where would I stay?

"Here," said Madeline, handing me a business card. "The physical therapy center at the naval base is a ten-minute drive from here. Jennifer, who I saw after my surgery, is wonderful. I'm sure you'll like her."

"Thanks." I sat back down at the table while Madeline finished cooking breakfast. "I'm not sure when Dutch will be back."

Madeline poured two cups of coffee, handed one to me, and then sat down at the table, next to me. "You're welcome to stay here as long as you'd like."

"I don't want to be an imposition, but..."

"You're not an imposition. The guest house sits empty most of the time, and once everyone else leaves later today, it'll be much too quiet around here."

"Everyone is leaving today?" That made me feel even worse about staying on. I had an apartment in New York City that my parents had purchased several years ago and then deeded to me when I retired from the Air Force. I spent so little time there, though. For the last two years, it seemed as though the missions I'd been assigned were back-to-back. I'd been traveling nonstop up until I was shot and wound up in the hospital, fearing I might be paralyzed.

When I was released, Dutch took me to the condo he'd rented near the hospital. From there we'd gone to his place near Langley. Maybe it was time for me to think about returning to New York and resuming physical therapy there.

"Eat," said Madeline, pointing to my untouched breakfast. "You can solve the world's problems once you have food in your stomach."

"You're very astute," I said between mouthfuls of scrambled eggs.

Madeline laughed. "I was married to a military man for over forty years. I've learned to *glean*."

I laughed too.

"It's such a beautiful day," Madeline said, looking out the window. "Would you be up for a walk later?"

"I'd love it."

When the rest of the team left, Madeline took me to downtown Annapolis which, in its center, had open docks for boats traveling up and down the Chesapeake Bay. Even though the days right around Christmas were cold, with the warmer weather, many of the docks' tie-ups were full of boats still decked out in holiday regalia.

"I'm sorry we missed the boat parades, but there will be music, food, and fireworks at the City Dock on New Year's Eve," said Madeline.

I doubted I'd be here since it was still four days away, but either way, it sounded like fun and I said so.

The historic downtown was so warm and inviting, with carolers still strolling its brick streets. Lights and wreaths were hung on the countless eighteenth-century homes as well as on the small shops lining both sides of Main Street.

"Hungry?" Madeline asked.

Surprisingly, I was.

"How's the Federal House sound?"

"Anything is fine with me."

"It's been around since the seventeen hundreds, so it's safe to say it's good."

I followed her inside.

"They say that many of our founding fathers sat in this same room, before it was a restaurant, of course. Marchand and I used to have conversations about the things that happened here that forged our country as we know it."

Mantis would love this place. He revered American history, particularly anything to do with the constitution he, like everyone who worked for K19, vowed to protect and uphold.

"The cornerstone out front says seventeen-thirty, is that right?" I asked.

"Sure is," said a man approaching our table, who introduced himself as the owner and greeted Madeline like a lifelong friend.

I sat back and listened to the two of them talk about Marchand Godet and what a fine man he'd been. It was obvious that Madeline's love affair with her husband had never ended even though they were married for over forty years.

"We miss seeing you both," the man said before excusing himself.

"You miss him a lot."

"I do. March and I had a wonderful life full of grand adventures coupled with an easy enjoyment of day-to-day life. We didn't agree about everything, not by a long shot, but we learned to compromise and, above all else, respect one another."

That's what I'd once wanted with Mantis, but it hadn't worked. What was missing? The mutual respect? The willingness to compromise? And was that on his part or mine?

"When you meet your one true love, you know it. Even if you try to tell yourself he isn't it, somewhere deep in your heart, you know he is."

I smiled. "Are you trying to tell me something?"

Madeline patted my hand. "Only you know the answers, my dear. Now, what sounds good for lunch?"

We shared clam chowder, crab cakes, and fish and chips. By the time we finished eating, my stomach hurt, but my heart was warm.

"Thank you for today," I said as we wandered the shops of the historic downtown, buying things we both agreed we didn't need but couldn't pass up.

"Thank you for joining me." Madeline put her arm through mine. "I hope you'll come back and visit often."

Why hadn't it ever been like this with my own mother? I couldn't remember a single time the two of us spent the afternoon shopping or talking over a two-hour lunch.

Maybe it was because my parents, like Marchand and Madeline, were so in love that they forgot to share their affection with their daughter.

When I felt my eyes tearing up, I shook myself. There was no point in thinking about things that couldn't be changed. Instead, I'd focus on the future and try to figure out what that meant.

7

Dutch

"Where are you headed when we get back?" I asked Mantis.

"I guess that's up to Doc. I have a call scheduled with him after the briefing in the morning."

"Are you going to take some time off?"

"I doubt it."

"Why not?"

"What the hell else am I going to do, Dutch? Does it look to you like I have any kind of a life outside of work?"

I understood exactly what Mantis meant. I'd been in the same position often enough in my life. I wanted to tell him I empathized, but since it was my fault Mantis' life was so empty, at least romantically, I kept my damn mouth shut.

There were so many times in the last ten years when I'd been the third wheel, the odd man out, the stray without anywhere to go and anything to do unless it was with Mantis and Alegria.

When we were all together at the academy, it had been easy. Our lives were so structured, and since all of us were on the same schedule, Mantis and Alegria were good about including me in whatever plans they had.

Cadets were required to live in the dorms all four years, and our daily schedule didn't allow for much free time. Days were filled with classes and military training. Mealtimes were inflexible, and after dinner, our time was divided between the commandant and the dean.

As the commander in charge of our military training, the commandant "owned us" up until twenty-one hundred hours, when we became the property of the dean—which meant quiet study time.

The academics at the academy were rigorous. In fact, if it hadn't been for Mantis and Alegria's tutoring, I probably would have been on academic probation most of my time there.

As we became upperclassmen, we were afforded more free time, but it certainly wasn't generous. There were still curfews and room checks, and if a cadet fell behind in his or her studies, either academic or military, they could be confined to their quarters.

It wasn't until Mantis and Alegria went off to pilot training in Texas and I was sent overseas for my first assignment, that I realized how much I relied on the two of them for a social life.

I'd dated some while at the academy, but I preferred to be with Mantis and Alegria, partially because the three of us were best friends, and partially because I had loved Alegria, heart and soul, for just as long as Mantis had. I got jealous, like anyone would, but I had the choice to stay away, and I didn't. Even then I'd take whatever Alegria was willing to give.

It was as true today as it had always been. Would she ever love me the way she loved Mantis? I doubted it. Was that good enough? I told myself it was, but for how long? For the rest of my life?

"Deep in thought," Mantis commented.

"Like you, I have a lot to figure out when I get back."

Mantis scrubbed his face with his hand. "I can't do this, Dutch."

"What?"

"I can't be your wingman in your relationship with Alegria."

"I get that," I said, even though that's what I'd always been for him.

8

Mantis

I prepared myself for the argument Doc and I would have about when I'd be ready for another assignment. Tomorrow wouldn't be too soon for me, but I knew Doc would insist I take time off.

For what, though? Like I'd told Dutch, other than work, my life was empty. I could spend a couple of days with my family in Connecticut since I didn't show up for Christmas, but after that, what would I do?

When I came home after being in Afghanistan for so many months, my plan had been to try to work things out with Alegria. I'd had no intention of taking on anything other than flying for at least a year. Maybe longer.

When Doc offered me the K19 partnership, I turned him down, not knowing whether I could commit to the firm when what I wanted to do more than anything was retire.

Within days, everything had changed. Alegria refused to talk to me about anything other than work. K19 had an op that required every team member's support, including mine, and then at the end of that mission, Alegria had been shot.

Dutch had been the one to find her, barely alive, in the woods that night. Even then, he hadn't let on that the two of them were together.

"You and Dutch head home," Doc said when we reached the end of our call.

What should be a simple thing to do, wasn't. Where was my home? I had a lease on a condo in Santa Barbara, but was that home? In the absence of any-where else to go, it would have to work until I figured out what I wanted to do next.

"Hey, Doc?"

"Still here."

"Is that partnership at K19 on the table?"

"Holding it open just for you."

"I think I'd like to take you up on it."

"Glad to hear. You're part of the K19 team family no matter what, but having you official is what we'd all prefer."

We talked about what was involved in terms of paperwork, and what kind of money I could plan to bring in. The next step was for us to meet and finalize the deal.

"Once we're stateside, I'm going to Darien for a couple of days, and then I'll head to Santa Barbara."

"Sounds good. Say hello to your parents for me, and let me know when you're in town."

I thanked him and ended the call. I'd lucked out when, as a fledgling CIA agent, I was given my first assignment to work with Doc and the K19 team. They were honest, ethical, and as Doc had said, they were a family.

When I came out of the room where I'd made my call, Dutch was waiting.

"Transport is scheduled for thirteen hundred."

I checked my watch. That meant I had at least four hours to kill, and Mogadishu wasn't known for sightseeing.

"I have some travel plans to arrange. I'll meet you back at the airfield," I told him.

"I was thinking we could grab something to eat."

As much as I wanted to turn Dutch down, if I was going to be a K19 partner, that meant I was going to have to work with the man. Not just Dutch, Alegria too. I had to figure out a way to coexist with the two of them.

"Where are you headed?" Dutch asked when we sat at a table in the cafeteria.

"What do you mean?"

"You said you had travel plans to make."

"Right. Goin' to see the folks first and then out to Cali to meet with Doc."

"Does that mean you're coming on board?"

I nodded, and Dutch held out his hand.

"Congratulations," he said when I shook it. "I'm glad you changed your mind."

When I first came back from Afghanistan, I'd talked to Dutch about my plans to retire. I hadn't mentioned Alegria, but neither had Dutch.

"I'm sorry I didn't tell you."

"What's that?" I asked.

"I've known you a third of my life. More than that. I know you, Cassman, and I know what you're thinking."

"If that's true, you wanna explain why you didn't?"

"The truth?"

I nodded.

"I figured she'd change her mind."

"You thought I'd come back and Alegria would break things off with you."

This time Dutch nodded.

I leaned back in my chair. "You were wrong."

"How do we work this?" Dutch asked.

"You tell me, man. How many years were you in love with her and somehow managed to spend time with us when we were a couple. I figure you know how to do this better than I do."

"It's different."

"I don't think it is."

Dutch shrugged. "Time will tell. I just hope we can be friends again."

"There was never a time we weren't."

"There was never a time you didn't want to pummel me?" Dutch laughed.

"I didn't say that, did I?" I rubbed the back of my neck with my hand. "Listen. I was pissed, okay? For a lot of reasons. I'm not gonna lie and tell you that I don't wish you'd found someone else. Anyone else. But you didn't, and that's something I'm going to have to live with."

"I don't know what to say."

"Nothing to say. She and I ended things, and then I was gone for a long time. Neither of you knew when or if I was coming back. I should probably thank you for taking such good care of her, but I'm not a big enough man to do that yet." I pushed my chair back and stood. "Dutch, you've been a good friend to me for many years. Fuck, you just saved my life. But I can't talk about this anymore."

"Understood."

I turned to walk away, but stopped and looked over my shoulder. "This was the last conversation we're gonna have on the subject. It is what it is."

"Roger that," Dutch said as I left the room.

9

Alegria

"There's something I need to talk to you about," I said to Dutch when we'd gotten the niceties of our telephone conversation out of the way.

"Shit," I heard him murmur.

"Why did you say shit? You have no idea what I'm about to tell you."

"Sorry, go ahead."

I didn't have as much of a French accent after all the years I'd been living in the States, but it came out when I was angry. If things escalated, I reverted to speaking the language.

"Je rentre chez moi."

"To France?"

"Non! New York."

"I didn't realize you considered New York home."

"I have nowhere else to go."

Dutch took a deep breath. "Where are you now?"

"Where you left me."

"In Annapolis?"

I nodded.

"Alegria, are you still there?"

"Sorry. Yes. I'm still at the Godets'." As nice as Gunner's mother was, it wasn't just that I was still staying in their guest house; it was more that when the time came for me to leave, I didn't know where I'd go, and that left me feeling unsettled.

"There are other options."

"What? To live with you?"

"Isn't that what we've been doing?"

I stood and paced the room, cursing myself when I realized I was biting my nails.

"Can't this wait until I get back? We're flying into Reagan International. I'll be to you an hour after we land."

"We?"

"Mantis is flying from Reagan to Westchester."

"He's going to see his parents?"

"Manon?"

He so rarely called me by my given name, I didn't know what to think. "Yes?"

"Do you want to see him?"

"What do you mean?" I asked, barely above a whisper.

"Come to the airport. See him before he goes to Darien."

"Why?"

"Because I know you want to. Because you'll feel better after you've seen him, and he will too."

"I don't know."

"I'll send a car. We'll see you tomorrow afternoon."

"Dutch?"

"Yeah, sweetheart?"

"Thank you."

By the time the driver showed up at noon the following day, I'd changed my mind about going to the airport at least a dozen times. Poor Madeline had listened to me talk myself in and out of it.

"Go," she said, peering out the window when a car pulled in the driveway.

"I..."

"Just go." Madeline gave me a nudge toward the door.

"Thank you," I said, hugging her. "I know I haven't been the most gracious guest."

"You know what you are? You're a treasured friend who is welcome here anytime."

I thanked her again and opened the door when the driver knocked. Right before walking out, I turned around and kissed both of Madeline's cheeks.

"*Au revoir, mon amie.*"

As indecisive as I'd been before, once I was in the car, alone with the driver, it got much worse. Had Dutch told Mantis I was meeting them at the airport? If not, how would he react to seeing me there? Would he think I was there only to see Dutch?

More troubling was why I wanted to see him so badly, and why Dutch had suggested I come.

10

Dutch

"There's something I need to talk to you about," I said to Mantis and then laughed.

Mantis looked up from the book he was reading on his tablet. "What's funny?"

"Nothing really. Alegria started a conversation with me a couple of hours ago using those exact words, and I didn't react very well."

Mantis looked back down at his book.

"She's coming to the airport."

"Okay," he responded without looking up.

"To see you."

It was one of the hardest things I'd ever had to do, and if my instincts were right, things were going to get a hell of a lot harder for me in the very near future.

In the same way I often knew what Mantis was thinking, I could predict what Alegria was thinking too. When I'd heard the pain in her voice, the indecisiveness, I couldn't do anything but ask her to come to the airport. If she really wanted to be with me, she wouldn't have been talking about going "home" to New York.

She would've assumed, like I had, that we'd pick up where we'd left off before Christmas, and where I went, she would go too.

I'd gone as far as imagining the drive from Annapolis back to Newport News and where we'd stop along the way. When I realized I'd be back in time for New Year's Eve, I'd made plans for that too.

Now I had to make different plans. Ones that a single man would make.

11

Mantis

What the fuck was Dutch up to? "You know, for someone in love, you sure as hell push her in my direction a lot."

"It isn't that."

I looked up from my book and met Dutch's eyes.

"What is it, then?"

"We've been best friends for close to fifteen years. At the end of the day, that's what's most important to me."

"You can't force it. People grow apart, Dutch. Whether you and Alegria are together or not, our friendship may never be the same as it once was. That's life."

When Dutch shrugged and looked out the window, I looked back at my tablet. I'd read the same two paragraphs several times and hadn't retained a single word. There was no point in trying to read when all I could think about was the beautiful French girl who had captured my eighteen-year-old heart.

I rested my head against the seat back and closed my eyes. I could hardly remember my life before she came waltzing into it.

**

Her ebony-black hair was pulled back into the tight bun required by Air Force regulations, highlighting her mesmerizing, almond-shaped, gray-blue eyes. She looked terrified, and rightly so.

Our squadron commander had briefed us on her arrival a week ago. Manon Mondreau had attended the *École Spéciale Militaire de Saint-Cyr* in Northwest France for a year, but was transferring to the Air Force Academy as a C3C, or third-class cadet, like my best friend, Tom Miller, and I were.

"Hi, I'm Gehring Cassman," I said once her official introduction to the squadron was over. I'd slowly made my way closer to her so I could be the first to meet her personally. Tom, of course, was right on my heels.

"Manon Mondreau," she said, shaking the hand I'd extended.

"This is Tom," I said, wishing I could just ignore him but knowing that would be rude.

"Cadet Miller? A word," said the commander.

I said a silent prayer of thanks that Tom had been called away and I could talk to Manon alone.

"If you have any questions, want a tour, pretty much anything, just let me know."

When she whispered, "*Merci,*" and then smiled, my heart practically stopped.

* * *

God, I'd loved her. Still did, if I was honest.

I opened my eyes, shook my head, and tried once again to focus on my book. I glanced over at Dutch, who appeared to have fallen asleep, and breathed a sigh of relief. If he were awake, he'd ask me what I was thinking about. That's just how Dutch was.

I looked out of my own window at the clouds we were flying through, already anxious to get back into the cockpit. Thanks to Doc Butler, it wouldn't be long before I was. Doc had left a message earlier, saying that Onyx was bringing one of the K19 planes to the airfield and I was welcome to fly it to Westchester.

I'd immediately confirmed, and when I asked about filing the flight plan, Doc told me it had already been taken care of.

There was really nothing like flying a plane—except sex—and that was totally different, although no less exhilarating.

Sex. Jesus. Now was not the time for me to think about sex. It had been way too long, longer than I wanted to admit even to myself, since I sank into the soft body of a warm woman. The truth was, I hadn't been with anyone since the last time Manon and I were together. I couldn't bring myself to imagine being intimate with anyone but her.

There was no more beautiful woman in the world as far as I was concerned. Everything about her heated me up. It wasn't just her body I lusted after; it was her soul. Manon was complicated, sure, but she was also kind, lively, funny, and absolutely badass.

Her eyes could tell me a chapters-long story without her having to say a word. Her every expression was etched into my memory. I knew when she was tired, but not sleepy. I knew when she was frustrated, when anyone else would think she was angry. Her smile lit up the darkest recesses of my soul, bathing me in the healing light only she could give me.

The thought of never holding her naked body in my arms again made me come close to losing my shit and driving my hand through the plane's window.

Agony. That's how being without her felt. The worst agony I could ever imagine times ten thousand. Would the countless memories we'd made together ever fade, or would they haunt me for the rest of my damn life?

And Dutch? He wanted us to be the happy three-some we'd never really been. When the situation was reversed and I was with Alegria, Dutch had probably been as miserable as I was now, but he'd hidden it well.

Could I be that man? Could I sit at the table with them, listen to her tell a story, and stop myself from pulling her into my arms and kissing her?

Could I watch as Dutch touched her, held her hand, stroked her cheek with his finger? What would I do if she and Dutch kissed? The idea alone made me want to kill him.

I shook my head and looked over at Dutch. He was no longer asleep. His dark, hooded eyes fixated on me, letting me know he knew exactly what I'd been thinking about.

12

Alegria

This was a terrible idea. Why had I agreed to it? It was so much easier when I just avoided Mantis. Intentionally being here to welcome him home felt... awkward. Should I approach Dutch first? If Dutch kissed me, how would Mantis feel?

"*Argh,*" I growled and continued to pace the floor of the USO lounge.

"Alegria?" I heard someone say, and turned around to see Shiver Whittaker walking in with a woman who looked vaguely familiar.

"Hi," I said, approaching them.

We cheek-kissed.

"This is my sister, Darrow. Darrow, meet Alegria. She's with K19."

"It's nice to meet you," said Darrow, who then looked at her brother. "Do you ever go anywhere without running into someone you know?"

"Rarely."

Something was up with Shiver; I could sense it, but with his sister here, I wouldn't ask.

"Where are you headed?" I asked Darrow instead.

"My brother is dropping me off to stay with friends in DC. Where he's going is always a mystery."

"Why are you here?" Shiver asked.

"Dutch and Mantis are flying in from Mogadishu."

He raised a brow.

"Don't ask," I said, looking away and then pulling out my phone when it vibrated. "They've landed."

"Tell them we're here."

"Do you have plans? Maybe we could all have dinner?" Darrow suggested.

Shiver scowled but then nodded, making me feel as though I wasn't the only one in the room out of sorts.

"My friends won't be back until tomorrow," Darrow explained, "but my brother couldn't wait another day to dump me here."

"It wasn't like that," Shiver murmured, but I got the impression that's exactly how it was.

"Well, hello," I heard Dutch say, and spun around to see the two men who had been my friends, my lovers, my everything for so many years. On their own, they took my breath away. Seeing them side by side, I nearly fainted.

They were close to the same height, over six feet, but Mantis was more muscular. His thick forearms looked tanned, contrasted against his starched, white shirt-sleeves that were rolled up to just below his elbows. I thought I saw the hint of a tattoo I wasn't aware he had just beneath the folds. His deep blue eyes penetrated mine so intensely, I had to look away.

Instead, I looked over at Dutch, who smirked more than smiled.

"Get over here, girl," he said in a teasing voice.

I walked into his arms and was relieved when all he did was hug and release me.

"Hi," I said to Mantis and tentatively stepped closer to him.

We hugged as awkwardly as I'd anticipated, and then I stepped back from him.

"You know Darrow," I heard Shiv say, and was surprised when both Dutch and Mantis took turns hugging her in a far warmer way than I'd experienced.

"I've just invited Alegria to dinner," his sister told us. "Can you join us?"

I hadn't exactly accepted Darrow's invitation, but when I saw Mantis nod and Dutch look at me hopefully, I murmured my agreement.

The only person who looked as uncomfortable as I felt was Shiver, and he looked more anxious than annoyed like I was.

Two hours later, my back hurt, but not as badly as my ego. It seemed both Dutch and Mantis had endless questions for Darrow, and all but ignored me. I'd been ready to leave at least an hour ago, but Dutch didn't seem like he would be anytime soon.

"You okay?" Mantis asked.

"I'm tired and my back hurts," I told him, although I wasn't sure he'd heard me since he was looking at his phone.

I pushed my chair away from the table. If Dutch couldn't pay enough attention to notice, I'd see if there were any flights to New York I could catch tonight. I'd be just as alone in my Manhattan apartment as I felt here.

"Sorry," I heard Mantis say and then felt his hand on my arm. "I needed to double-check the flight plan."

"You're flying to Westchester?"

Mantis raised his eyebrow. "I am."

"Dutch told me," I explained. "How are your parents?"

"Getting older, like we all are, but still as active as ever."

"And your brother?"

"He and Theresa just had their fourth. A girl, I think."

I shook my head and rolled my eyes.

"What?"

"A girl...you think."

He shrugged. "You can blame my short-term memory loss on the Somalis."

"It isn't like you to blame anyone else for your shortcomings."

He was looking at his phone again, which was my cue to walk away.

"Wait," he said. "I was looking for a photo."

Mantis handed me his phone, and I looked at the picture of his two nephews and two nieces. The fourth was a girl, judging by the pink blanket she was swaddled in.

"I'm guessing you don't know her name."

Mantis smiled and shook his head. "In my defense, I'm heading there to see them now. That should count for something. By the way, when I get back, I'm signing a partnership agreement with K19. Will that be a problem?"

"Not at all. Congratulations," I murmured, casting my gaze toward Dutch, who seemed enthralled by his conversation with Darrow and Shiver.

"He's looked over a couple of times," Mantis whispered.

My head spun to look at him. "What?"

"He's giving you space."

I huffed and then wished I hadn't.

"Better put, he's giving us space."

"What for?" I asked.

"To be friends...I think."

I folded my arms, looked over at Dutch, and then back at Mantis. "I'm going to New York."

"When?"

"Tonight, if I can get a flight."

Mantis' eyes bored into mine. "Why, Flygirl?"

I shrugged, and my eyes filled with tears. "Sorry," I said, wiping at them. "I'm not feeling myself."

"How's the recovery going?"

"Far too slowly."

"What's the status of your medical clearance?"

I looked away from him, hating how much of a *girl* I was being in that moment. "Stalled," I whispered.

I hadn't told anyone that the last time I saw the doctor, I didn't have feeling in the sole of my right foot. Not Dutch, not Doc, and not my parents.

Mantis pulled me back into the chair and sat next to me. "What's happening?"

"Isolated neuropathy."

Mantis nodded. "Where?"

"Right plantar more than left, but there are issues with both."

"I see," he murmured, running his finger back and forth over his lips.

"I need to resume physical therapy."

"Have you been in the air?"

I shook my head.

"Why not?"

I rolled my eyes for the second time. "Getting me into a plane hasn't exactly been a priority for K19."

"I'm sure it will be soon," he murmured, studying me.

"You're making me uncomfortable."

Mantis nodded.

"You're doing it on purpose?"

It took him a few seconds to respond. "I like looking at you," he leaned forward and whispered. "I can't help it."

A shiver ran up my spine as I remembered the very first time he'd said those words to me.

* * *

"I'm failing aero," he'd said, slamming his books down onto the table near me.

I'd come to the library to study for the same class he was complaining about, but not because I was failing. As it was, I had the best grade in the class and intended to keep it that way. If I had a prayer of getting a pilot-training recommendation from the *École Spéciale Militaire de Saint-Cyr*, my grades as well as my military record from the Air Force Academy had to be as perfect as I could possibly achieve. Even then, I'd be faced with almost unsurmountable opposition in the form of one *Général de Brigade Aérienne* Pierre Mondreau—my father.

One would think he'd be proud that I wanted to follow in his footsteps and become a pilot, but from the first I'd told him it was what I wanted to do, he'd adamantly refused to discuss it further.

With his endorsement, I would've been accepted regardless of my grades. Without it, I had a better chance of becoming the queen of France.

I looked up at Gehring. He was seated across from me, his head resting on his hand, staring.

"What?" Did I have something on my face?

"I like looking at you. I can't help it."

I smiled. "I'm not sure if that is a good or bad thing."

"It's a very good thing. At least for me. I could do it all day and night."

It wasn't unlike Gehring to flirt. Tom did too. But weren't the three of us friends? Most of the time, I thought they were both teasing, but sometimes, especially when Gehring and I were alone, I found myself wishing he was seriously interested in me in the same way I was in him.

"Hey, Gehring," said another one of the female cadets, who walked by but then circled back and stood next to the chair he was seated in.

"Hey, Mel," he said, not bothering to look up.

"A few of us are going to Cowboys later. We thought maybe you and Tom would want to come along."

"Yeah, maybe," he said, still not looking up.

"Okay. See you later."

"I hate it when they do that," he said once the cadet had walked away.

"When they do what?"

"Act like you're not even sitting there."

I shrugged. "It doesn't bother me."

"It does, but you know why they do it, right?"

I shook my head.

"Because there isn't a single woman at this academy who is even half as beautiful as you are."

* * *

"You're still the most beautiful woman I've ever known," Mantis said, as though he could read my thoughts. "But you're so much more than that."

"Mantis—"

"No, I get it. You're with Dutch now. I can't say things like that anymore."

I nodded, but inside, the idea of never hearing words like those pass through Mantis' lips broke my heart.

"So what about getting you back in the pilot's seat?" he asked.

"I don't know. It might be…"

"What?"

"Impossible."

13

Dutch

I watched Alegria with Mantis and came to a decision. Whether either of them could admit they wanted me to, I had to walk away and give them a chance to see what was so obvious to me. They loved each other, and the only thing stopping them from falling into each other's arms was Alegria's relationship with me.

I would've been better off leaving before I even saw her. That way, she could be pissed off at me instead of sneaking glances my way every now and then with a guilty look on her face.

There wasn't a time I could remember when Alegria had looked at me the way she was looking at Mantis now. Everything between them had always been easy, up until they fought. Even then it was the depth of the passion they had for each other that made their disagreements so volatile.

My chest hurt when I thought back on how it was when they'd make up. They couldn't keep their hands off each other, and while they did their best not to make me feel uncomfortable, then, like I was doing now, I'd make up some excuse why I had to leave.

I took my phone out of my pocket and sent a message to Doc. There must be some kind of op that would require my help.

No matter what the mission was that Doc came back with, I would accept it. It didn't matter how dangerous.

Even if I got hurt, it couldn't possibly feel worse than what I was experiencing right then, watching Mantis and Alegria fight the overpowering attraction they shared.

14

Mantis

The sadness I saw and felt in Alegria was something I could empathize with. Back when I was still in the Air Force, I'd needed surgery for a hiatal hernia. Even though it had been done laparoscopically, it took me longer than I'd anticipated to get back in the cockpit. At the time, I'd been air wing operations officer and was required to deploy with my squadron whether I could fly or not.

The medical officer's reluctance to clear me, he'd said, was due to his fear that I wasn't recovered enough to perform the anti-G straining maneuver, or AGSM, while in the aircraft. Not having adequate body strength in my abdomen meant I'd be unable to perform the maneuver, which could result in a G-force induced loss of consciousness, otherwise known as G-loc.

For several days, I was unsure when I would be cleared to fly again, if ever. The idea that my career as a fighter pilot might come to an abrupt end had terrified me. Flying defined me, as it did Alegria.

"I'm sorry," I whispered, not knowing what else to say.

She shrugged one shoulder and tried to put on a brave front, but I saw right through it.

"What are the two of you so deep in conversation about?"

"Alegria was telling me about her neuropathy," I answered. As soon as the words left my mouth, I caught the look that told me she hadn't discussed this with Dutch.

My friend didn't react other than to look into Alegria's eyes. "It's rough," he murmured.

"There's a program at NYU I've been researching," she said, looking back and forth between us. "They've had promising results. Although no one will be back until the beginning of the second semester, in mid-January."

"That's not so long away," I encouraged.

"How long has it been since you've flown?"

Alegria's question was rhetorical. I got that. I also recognized that it wasn't very many hours ago I'd been anxious to get back in the air, and soon would be.

"Sorry," we both heard Dutch mutter, looking at his phone.

"What?" Alegria asked before I could.

"A message from Doc. Would you excuse us for a minute?" he asked me, already maneuvering Alegria away.

I watched them walk toward the restaurant's entrance and then moved seats so I was closer to Shiver and Darrow.

"Evidently, everyone has a mystery," she said, scowling at her brother, who didn't respond. "Doesn't it get tiresome?"

"It's the life we chose," I answered.

She nodded. "I guess dinner is over. Excuse me."

Shiver and I watched her walk in the direction of the ladies' room.

"Anything I can help with?" I asked once she was out of earshot.

"Thanks, but I don't think so," Shiver answered.

I nodded. "Let me know if you change your mind."

Shiver nodded in return. "What about you?"

"Come again?"

"Anything I can help with?"

I looked over my shoulder to where Dutch and Alegria were deep in conversation. "I don't think there's much hope."

Shiver shook his head. "You're wrong."

"What makes you think so?"

"Alegria loves you; she always will."

"What if that isn't enough?"

"I'm wondering that myself, mate."

I had no idea what Shiver was referring to. Regardless, we obviously weren't talking about Alegria and me any longer.

15

Alegria

"What's happening?" I asked when Dutch led me out the front door of the restaurant.

"I don't know all the details yet, but there's an op."

"How soon will you be deploying?"

"Right away. Doc's arranging transport to California as we speak."

"I'll go straight to Manhattan, then."

Dutch cupped my cheek with his palm. "I wish I didn't have to leave tonight."

"Me too."

When he leaned down and kissed me, I wrapped my arms around his waist. As I had so many times before, I wished I felt the same level of passion for him as I always had for Mantis. No matter how much I wanted it, I'd never been able to force it.

"I gotta go," Dutch said, taking my arms from his waist. "Do you want me to give you a lift back to the terminal?"

"No, I can catch a cab. Go if you need to."

"I'm sorry," he said again before pulling me against him and kissing me a second time. "I'll call when I know more."

I waved as he climbed into a waiting car. Was I imagining that he was saying more than goodbye for the duration of the mission, or had Dutch just said farewell to me forever?

When I went back inside, I saw Mantis and Shiver alone at the table. I was about to turn around and leave when Mantis waved me over.

"I'm off," Shiver said, standing and kissing each of my cheeks. "If you need anything…"

I nodded and saw Darrow was already near the door. "Thanks. Please say goodbye to your sister for me."

"Well," I began after Shiver had left. "I suppose it's time for me to go too."

"Where?"

"Manhattan, I guess." I sighed.

"You don't sound excited about the prospect."

"You want the truth?"

Mantis nodded. "Always."

"I don't have anywhere else to go."

"You could come home with me."

"To Darien?"

"Why not? How long has it been since you've seen my family? I know they'd love to see you."

"Wouldn't it be...uncomfortable?"

"You mean because you're with Dutch now?"

I shrugged. "More that you and I aren't together."

"It'll give us time to practice."

I laughed. "Practice what?"

"Being friends."

Faced with going to a cold and empty apartment where I hadn't spent more than a week in God knew how long, or going to visit Mantis' family, whom I adored, my choice was easy to make.

"Sure, I'd love to go with you."

Mantis' smile made my toes curl. He was right about us needing practice being friends, given right now I wanted to fall into his arms and never leave.

16

Mantis

Just because Alegria had agreed to go home with me didn't mean anything between us had changed. I'd joked that it would give us practice being friends, but truthfully, I couldn't stand the idea of saying goodbye to her so soon.

For the first time since I came back from Afghanistan, we'd had the kind of conversation we so often used to.

I understood her frustration as well as her concern. In the same position, I doubted I'd be handling it as well as Alegria was, but that was the way it had always been.

There were plenty of times I'd teased her for being French, but I always meant it as a compliment. I wondered sometimes if I'd find the women I'd seen in France as captivating if I'd never met Alegria. It wasn't that I was attracted to them in the same way I was to her— not even the slightest bit. Instead, I watched their mannerisms, their grace, the way they could turn a pout into the sexiest damn thing I'd ever seen, and then light up all those around them with their smile.

Alegria moved like a gazelle—thin, graceful, and quick. Her mind moved that way too, as though it went from zero to sixty in a split second.

Unlike other French women I'd known, who picked at their food, my Flygirl had always had a hearty appetite, yet she stayed fit with a workout schedule that had often intimidated Dutch and me.

* * *

"Are you going to the gym today?" Dutch asked as we walked across the marble tiles of the Air Force Academy's Terrazzo. Named for the checkerboard of marble strips that made up the area's walkways, the large pavilion was surrounded by the main buildings in what was known as the cadet area.

As freshmen, or doolies, Dutch and I had had to run on those marble strips during passing periods, slinging our backpacks over one shoulder like all the fourth-class cadets were required to do. In the winter, the marble became slick, resulting in more than one cadet taking a tumble every day.

Now, as third-class cadets, or sophomores, we were no longer required to run or hold our backpacks a certain way. Instead, we were being trained to be the leaders and mentors of those who came after us.

"Hello?" said Dutch, waving his hand in front of my face.

"What?"

"I asked if you were going to the gym."

"Nah. I've got a big test tomorrow that I need to study for. If I'm done in time, I'll go later."

"Chickenshit," said Dutch, poking me. "You're just intimidated by Frenchie's workout routine."

"Don't call her that; she hates it. And you're wrong. I need to study."

"Yeah, well, I need to say a few prayers that I pass my PT test tomorrow." Dutch pointed at the cadet chapel that sat on the west side of the Terrazzo.

It was both the most recognizable building at the United States Air Force Academy and the most visited man-made tourist attraction in the state of Colorado. The aluminum, glass, and steel structure featured seventeen spires that shot one hundred and fifty feet into the sky like jets on a vertical ascent.

After graduation, many of the newly commissioned second lieutenants got married there before leaving for their first assignment.

"Tell you what, you go pray, and I'll go study, and maybe later you, me, and Manon can meet up."

"Gotta love a girl who can kick your ass," Dutch muttered, laughing as he walked away.

* * *

Dutch had been right, Alegria could've kicked my ass then, and probably still could. It was only one of ten thousand things I loved about her. Or that I used to love about her. She wasn't mine to love anymore. She was Dutch's now, and I had to respect the man who had always showed me the utmost consideration.

As hard as it was going to be to finally let her go, what choice did I have? I'd destroyed every chance we'd had to make it work. She'd warned me again and again that if I didn't listen, didn't put her first for once in our relationship, she would leave me for good. It wasn't as though I called her bluff. I'd left because I had a mission I needed to complete. It wasn't a choice for me even though she insisted it was.

Now that the mission was over, it was too late. On top of it, I knew that if I had to do it all over again, I'd make the same decisions. I owed it to my family. I'd wished then, like I wished now, that she understood, but she hadn't, and no amount of wishing would change that.

17

Dutch

It felt like I'd been punched in the gut, but I knew, deep in my heart, that I was doing the right thing by leaving, even if it meant lying about a mission I hadn't yet been assigned. I'd asked the driver to pull into the parking lot across from the restaurant and park. From there I saw Mantis and Alegria leave, their body language telling me everything I needed to know to confirm I was doing the right thing.

That Alegria was leaving with Mantis was confirmation enough. There was a chance he was simply giving her a ride back to the terminal so she could catch a flight to JFK, but something told me that wasn't what was going on. I'd bet anything that Mantis had asked her to fly to Westchester with him, and they were headed to the airfield.

I considered, only for a moment, asking the driver to follow them, but I didn't. Instead, I told the man he could go ahead and take me to the long-term parking lot where my own vehicle sat waiting for my long and lonely drive back to my empty house in Newport News. Alegria wasn't the only woman I'd ever loved, just the one I loved the most.

Before Mantis left for his final mission to Afghanistan; before I learned that he and Alegria had called it quits; before she called me from a local bar, crying and begging me to meet her there—I'd had someone else in my life.

Just like Mantis chose the mission over Alegria, I'd chosen Alegria over Malin.

She hadn't protested like Alegria had with Mantis; she'd just accepted my choice.

"She needs you," she'd said that night. "Go."

Every call I'd made to her after that night, every text, and every email I'd sent had gone unanswered.

It was no different than what Mantis had gone through when he returned from his mission and Alegria refused to talk to him.

There was no chance for Malin and me after what I'd done that night. I'd known that before I walked out the door. As far as being lonely, I had no one to blame but myself.

18

Mantis

"This is the plane Doc sent?"

"Yep. Looks that way," I answered, as surprised as Alegria was. Before us sat a Cirrus SF50 Vision Jet.

"When did K19 acquire it?"

I had no idea. With a price tag of two million bucks easy, the plane didn't compromise a damn thing, and evidently, K19 hadn't either.

As we approached the aircraft, I opened the single door on the left side of the plane. The bifold design opened to reveal a good-sized entry area.

"Go ahead," I said to Alegria, motioning for her to take the front co-pilot seat.

"Wow." She ran her hands over the supple leather. "This is something else."

I agreed as I got situated. The jet had a lot of head and shoulder room and a windscreen that was divided in the middle. The forward visibility was amazing while the side view was nothing short of spectacular.

The avionics suite featured two big fourteen-inch displays up front while a step below and closer to me and Alegria, were three touch-controller displays that had been mounted sideways.

"Look at these," Alegria said, pointing to the side-sticks on the left and right that traveled fore and aft like a more conventional yoke. "It's like a dream."

I nodded, working my way through the preflight checks only to realize that most of it had been automated.

"I could get used to this," I murmured. I initiated the start sequence and watched as the system ran its own series of checks on everything from TAWS to fire suppression. I moved the dial from the OFF position to RUN, and the single engine started itself.

"You can see everything," Alegria commented on our forward taxi visibility.

I nodded again and waited for clearance to take off.

Soon we were in the air. The view was amazing, and I wasn't talking about the one outside of the aircraft. I watched Alegria study the touch controllers, customizing the views as though she were flying the plane herself. I'd give anything to let her, but even if I broke the rules and did, I knew she wouldn't accept my offer.

She sat back in her seat and looked out the oval-shaped windows at the clouds below us.

"Hey."

She smiled. "Hey."

It felt so much like old times I almost reached over and took her hand in mine. This was what I meant by practicing. I had to get used to not taking her hand, not kissing her, not climbing in bed next to her, and not feeling her naked body under mine.

I looked away, silently cursing how wrong it had gone between us, and knowing I only had myself to blame. All she'd wanted was for me to choose her over the mission, and I hadn't been able to.

"The doctor said I might not be able to fly again."

I heard her even though she was looking the other way.

"What do you think?"

"Over my dead body."

I smiled. "That's my girl." Only she wasn't, was she? She was Dutch's girl now.

I couldn't see her face, so I didn't know if she'd caught my gaff and ignored it, or if she simply hadn't heard me.

Our estimated time en route, or ETE, was one hour and fifty minutes. There were no storms on the horizon, and Manon "Alegria" Mondreau was seated in the plane, next to me. There was a time I would've taken it all for granted, other than the jet we were flying. Now, it was a situation I might never find myself in again.

"I can help."

"What's that?"

"I can help you get medical clearance."

"Is bribery involved?"

I laughed. "No, but hard work might be."

"What are you proposing?"

"The Cirque d'Alegria."

"A circus?"

"Yeah, that didn't work, did it? Um, how about the Flygirl Olympics?" It's what we'd called it back when I had my own surgery and was unable to fly—the Praying Mantis Olympics. She'd pushed me damn hard back then, and it had paid off.

"Are you joking or are you serious?"

I wanted to reach over and soothe the hurt I saw in her brow. "I'm serious. You need to get your wings back."

"What if there's a mission?"

Her question stung, but I understood why she asked.

"Until you're cleared to get back in the air, I won't sign with K19."

"Why?"

"You'd do the same for me, wouldn't you?"

Alegria gave me a sideways glance. "Now I know you're kidding."

We'd always been fiercely competitive—textbook type A's—starting before we even knew we'd both been tagged for pilot training.

"In a moment of weakness maybe," I said.

Alegria laughed. God, I loved that sound.

"You helped me all those years ago."

"Things were different then," she said, the smile leaving her face.

"Not so different." I couldn't stop myself. I reached over and squeezed her hand with mine. "Let me help you."

She didn't pull her hand away, so I rubbed the back of it with my thumb. The too-intimate caress jarred her, and she moved her hand to her lap.

"Mantis—"

"Think about it."

19

Alegria

What was he doing to me, and why was he doing it? Was it only because I was with Dutch now? If he won me back, would he take me for granted and cast me aside like he had before? Would he take on the next mission that came his way once he knew I'd be waiting in his bed when, and if, he came home?

I couldn't do it. Not again.

"I shouldn't have done that. I'm sorry," I heard him say.

"What?"

"I shouldn't have touched your hand...that way."

I waited for him to continue.

"What I'm proposing is that we do this as friends. I promise not to cross the line again."

He'd barely sneaked a toe over it, but I knew what he meant. If I let him help me, we had to define boundaries and never cross them.

"Apology accepted."

"Does that mean you'll also accept my help?"

"It means I'll think about it." I looked over at him, but he wasn't looking at me. "Mantis?"

"Yeah?" he answered.

"I appreciate the offer so much."

"But..."

"No buts. I said I'd think about it. We don't even know what's involved yet."

We were both quiet the rest of the flight. As much as I didn't want to think about it, Mantis had broken my heart, and Dutch had been there to pull me through a very dark time of my life.

It didn't matter that I didn't feel the same passion for him that I felt for Mantis; I couldn't betray him. No more than I could risk Mantis breaking my heart all over again when the day came that I asked him not to go, but he left anyway.

The last time he had, I'd gone to a bar alone; something I never did. One glass of wine turned into another, and before I knew it, I'd polished off an entire bottle on my own. Worse, I hadn't eaten all day.

I hadn't blacked out, but what had happened that night was fuzzy. By the time Dutch arrived, I'd ordered the first glass of my second bottle, and by the time we left, we'd both had a lot more to drink.

Both of us drunk, I'd cried on his shoulder while Dutch had professed his undying, albeit unrequited, love for me.

I shook my head, wishing I hadn't left the house that night as much as I wished Mantis hadn't either.

20

Mantis

It was as though I could hear Alegria's thoughts, and each one was like a knife in my heart—one I'd put there myself. What had once been easy between us never would be again. We'd have moments, but a few minutes later, she'd remember that I'd left her when she asked me not to, and all the hurt would rise back to the surface. How many times could I say I was sorry?

I shook my head, acknowledging to myself that I'd never actually apologized, because I still wasn't sure I was sorry.

I wanted her back, though. Was it because she was with Dutch? Or was it because I'd finally gotten to the point in my life where I believed I might want the same things she did? The most important word in that thought was *might*. Even now I wasn't certain.

"Alegria," I murmured.

"What?"

"Nothing." It wasn't that I had anything in particular to say. It was that I was remembering the day she'd been given the call sign.

Sometimes, call signs could be almost disparaging, given at the comedic expense of the recipient. Like Stem, for example, who was given the name because after two beers, every part of his brain except the stem shut down. Or Frag, who was the social equivalent of a hand grenade. Alegria was the opposite.

Her call sign meant joy, happiness, and even freedom.

My first solo had been technically perfect. I told myself over and over again not to mess up, procedurally focused in my clinical approach. It was only after I saw the look on Manon's face when she climbed out of the aircraft after her first solo that I realized I'd done it all wrong.

What I saw that day was unadulterated joy. She'd slipped the surly bonds of earth, and flown. When the Portuguese pilot standing next to me murmured *alegria*, I immediately knew it should be her call sign.

When I stepped forward to spray her with the requisite champagne, I'd also bestowed on her the name most knew her by.

Where was that joy now? That happiness? That sense of freedom? Where was the fiery Flygirl I'd done battle with as we competed over everything from aeronautical engineering grades to PT scores?

That was the woman I wanted back. The last time I'd seen her was right before I told her I was taking the mission she'd asked me not to.

It was time to prepare for our descent and landing. Once we were on the ground, I planned to do everything I could to get that Alegria back. Even if she couldn't be mine.

My first landing of the SF50 was terrible. I flared too high, and my recovery was ham-handed, too. The entire approach was kin to Mr. Toad's Wild Ride, with multiple episodes of plus or minus ten-knot wind shear and squirrely, gusty winds once we arrived above the tarmac.

The good news was that even with the high flare, a short recovery, and a bit of a bounce, I still used less than half of the runway's length—in spite of, not because of, my brilliant technique.

"That...was...pitiful." Alegria was laughing so hard she could hardly speak, and soon I was too.

"Wait until you try to land this thing," I challenged.

"I wouldn't have to try very hard to do better than that," she said, wiping away her tears of laughter. "Jesus, how long did you say it had been since you flew?"

There she was, I thought to myself as she continued spewing trash talk. By the time she got her clearance to fly again, instead of getting a momentary glimpse of the woman she used to be before I took away her joy, I'd do everything in my power to give it back to her.

21

Alegria

"I had to see your face to believe you were really coming with him," Mantis' mother shouted as she ran down the steps of their front porch. "Come here, sweet girl."

When Minnie Cassman put her arms around me, I almost cried. It had been two years since I last saw Mantis' family, and until this moment, I didn't realize how much I'd missed their warmth and affection.

"Kip couldn't wait up any longer. He asked me to tell you he'd see you both in the morning."

"Hi, Mom," said Mantis as his mom wrapped him in a hug like she had me.

"I don't care how he managed it, I'm just glad you're here," said Minnie, linking her arm with mine as we walked up the steps. "I heard you had quite an ordeal. When was your surgery?"

I really didn't like to talk about it, or the gunshot that had necessitated it, but Minnie had a way of getting me to.

"I've been out of the hospital a little over a month. They couldn't operate right away. They had to wait until my condition stabilized." I told Minnie about my time in the ICU and about how rigorous physical therapy had been.

At one point, I looked over at Mantis, who looked stunned.

"What?" I asked.

"I didn't realize how bad it was," he said quietly.

"Well, it explains the neuropathy, I guess."

"What's this?"

Soon I was explaining what had happened at my last checkup, something I hadn't shared the details about with anyone.

"I've volunteered to help her get her medical clearance."

Minnie looked at her son with skepticism. "How will you do that?"

"I have healing powers," he joked.

Minnie's gaze fell on me. "You were always the one with healing powers."

His mom was talking about how hard I'd worked Mantis when he was in a similar position. However, his surgery had been so much less severe than mine. I should probably be thankful I could walk rather than lamenting the fact that I couldn't fly.

"Let's get you settled in," Minnie said, standing and pointing to my bag. "You probably want to get some sleep."

I looked at Mantis, hoping he'd clear things up for his mother.

"I think Alegria will be more comfortable in the guest room on this floor. I'll sleep upstairs."

Minnie looked between us. "Of course she would," she finally said. "Gehring, set her bag on the cedar chest, and I'll air the room out."

"Thank you," I mouthed to him.

"Gehring did tell you that Jonas and Theresa had another baby, right? A girl they named Alana. Isn't that beautiful?" Minnie was babbling while she turned down the guest room bed. "Get some rest, sweetheart," she said, kissing my cheek.

"Thank you," I said out loud, this time to Minnie. "I am very tired."

Had it only been ten hours since I was grappling with meeting Dutch and Mantis at the airport? Yet, here I was with him at his parents' house. How in the world had that happened?

I looked up at the ceiling, knowing sleep wouldn't come anytime soon, especially since Mantis was in the room right above mine.

22

Dutch

The call from Doc came when I stopped at a truck stop to get a cup of coffee. Serendipitously, he had a mission for me. One I had to leave for immediately.

"I got a call from the agency. There's a situation back in Mogadishu, and they're asking for K19 support."

"I'm in."

"Where are you now?" he asked.

"About an hour from Langley."

"Roger that. I'll arrange transport from there."

I hung up and breathed a sigh of relief that I'd dodged the bullet of walking into my house alone while the scent of Alegria still wafted through its closed-up rooms.

Before I got back on the road, I had one more call to make. I'd known Minnie Cassman since Mantis and I were teenagers; I knew she'd never be in bed before midnight.

"They arrived a little over an hour ago," Minnie told me.

"Good. I'll check back in a few days."

Things couldn't have worked out better if I'd planned it myself.

"Dutch?"

"Yeah?"

"You're like a second son to me, and I know you're hurting. Are you sure about going through with this?"

"I don't have any choice."

I had to give Mantis and Alegria time to figure out whether they still loved each other as much as I believed they did. The only way that could happen was if I was out of the picture for an extended period of time.

23

Mantis

I tossed and turned most of the night, unable to think about anything other than the way I'd felt earlier when I took Alegria's hand in mine. As brief as the moment had been, having my skin touch hers, rubbing my thumb over the back of her hand, filled me with longing.

I had to continue reminding myself that the road we were tentatively headed down would only bring hurt to us both. She and Dutch were together, and I had no business getting in the middle of their relationship, no matter how rocky it appeared to be.

What kind of man would I be if I seduced my best friend's girlfriend? I could justify it by saying Dutch had done the same to me, but he hadn't. Nothing had happened between them until Dutch was certain she and I had broken up.

I wished I could go back to our time in Mogadishu when Dutch had asked if I wanted him to take a step back so I could try to work things out with Alegria. I'd said no at the time, and now I was cursing myself for it.

"What the hell, Dutch?" I murmured into the darkness.

When I saw the sun on the horizon, I decided there was no point in staying in bed any longer. I got up and went downstairs to make a pot of coffee.

Once it was brewing, I walked into the living room and stood in front of the wall of family pictures. In the middle of all the high school yearbook shots, hung the photo of Ian, my older brother, taken the day he was sworn in as a firefighter for the city of New York.

I rolled my shoulders and took a deep breath. The pain of missing my brother never went away. I wasn't alone in that; my parents felt it too. Hell, everyone who'd ever known Ian, missed the hell out of him.

The coffee's aroma beckoned me back into the kitchen. On a day like today, when I'd gotten no sleep the night before, my body needed the caffeine.

"Mmm," I heard Alegria say from behind me. She took my breath away when I turned around and saw her standing in the doorway.

She was barefoot, wearing an Air Force t-shirt that fell almost to her knees. If I remembered right, she'd had it since our academy days.

"Is it almost ready?" she asked, opening the kitchen cupboard where my mother kept the coffee cups.

"Another minute or so," I said, turning my back on her and opening the refrigerator as much to cool off as to get out the milk. As it was, I was a breath away from picking her up, setting her cute butt on the kitchen counter, and kissing her good morning the way I longed to.

When I turned back around, she was right in front of me with two steaming cups of coffee in her hands. I poured a little milk in each, set the container back in the fridge, and took one cup from her.

"Still no sugar, right?"

Alegria sat down at the table and rolled her eyes.

"What?"

"It hasn't been that long."

Actually, it felt as though it had been an eternity since we'd shared a cup of coffee while the rest of the world still slept. I took a seat across the table from her and watched as she closed her eyes and took a sip.

"This is really good," she murmured. "You always did make a great pot of coffee."

"I hope that wasn't my only talent, Flygirl."

Alegria's cheeks pinkened and her eyes met mine. God, I wanted to take her hand, pull her to my lap, and kiss her harder than I ever had before.

"I heard we had a visitor," said my dad, coming into the kitchen at either the best or worst possible moment.

Alegria stood and hugged him. "Hey, Kip. How are you?"

"Better now that you're here," he said.

"Hey, Dad." I hugged my father after Alegria had.

"Missed you, son," he said, thumping me on the back. "You too, pretty girl."

Alegria smiled and sat back down.

"Can I get you a cup of coffee?"

My dad waved me off. "I can get it, Gehring. Take a seat."

"What's all the racket in my kitchen?" said my mother, joining us.

"I hope we didn't wake you." Alegria stood to kiss my mother's cheek.

"Of course you didn't. You know I'm always up with the hens."

I never understood why my mother used that expression; she'd never owned chickens in her life.

"Where do you keep these hens?"

"I love having you in my kitchen, even with your smart mouth." She pinched my cheek and then poured herself a cup of coffee as well. "I thought the two of you would sleep in today."

I met Alegria's gaze. "Some habits die hard I guess."

"You've both always been early risers."

Alegria didn't look particularly uncomfortable, but I wondered if our conversation was making her feel that way. My mother was talking as if the two of us were an old married couple.

"Who's hungry?" my mom asked, opening the refrigerator.

"I am," said Alegria, jumping up. "Can I help?"

"Always, sweet girl." My mother smiled at her with all the love I felt myself. How many times had she and my mom made breakfast in this kitchen? Countless.

"Got a minute, son?" my father asked.

"Of course." I followed him out to the front porch.

"Fill me in," he said once we were seated.

"On?"

"You and Miss Frenchie."

I laughed. "We're friends, and she hates being called that, Dad."

My father leaned forward and shook his head. "Where did I go wrong?"

I laughed again. "We're meant to be friends, that's it."

"Bullshit," my dad muttered before getting up to go back into the house. "Open your eyes, Gehring. The woman helping your mother make breakfast is head over heels in love with you. Do something about it before you lose her again."

"Dad, wait."

My father turned around.

"She's with Dutch now."

My dad looked left and right. "Nope. She's not. Unless he's hidin' around the corner."

"You know what I mean."

Kip walked back over to me. "And you know what I mean."

I stayed on the porch after my dad went inside. As much as I wished it were that simple, it wasn't. I couldn't be that man any more than I could be the man who could stand by their side as a couple.

"Breakfast is ready," Alegria said, coming out to join me on the porch. "Everything okay?"

I stood in front of her. "Not really."

"I shouldn't be here. I knew this was a bad idea."

"That isn't it," I said, reaching out to cup her cheek. "They're having a hard time accepting we aren't together anymore. To be honest, they aren't the only ones."

"Mantis—"

I took my hand away. "I get it, and I'm sorry. I promised not to cross the line, and I just did." I met her gaze. "Forgive me?"

24

Alegria

Before I opened the door to go back inside, I looked over my shoulder. "It isn't easy for me either."

I didn't stop in the kitchen. Instead, I went into the bathroom and splashed cold water on my face.

I'd almost kissed him. It was only his apology that had stopped me. If he hadn't said it, I would've put my hands on either side of his face and kissed him as hard as I knew he wanted to kiss me.

How in the hell were we going to keep this as "just friends"? We hadn't been together twenty-four hours, and I was ready to kiss him. Not just that—I was ready to crawl into bed next to him.

"Are you okay, sweetheart?" Minnie asked when I came back in and joined them at the table.

"Yeah. I'm fine, thanks. So, coach," I said, looking at Mantis. "You ready to hit the gym today?"

He smiled that million-kilowatt smile of his, and I was ready to go back and splash my entire body with cold water. *Heaven, help me.* Mantis was the sexiest man I'd ever known, and I was about to go to the gym with him and his too-short shorts and his too-tight t-shirts.

He pulled a piece of paper out of his pocket when we got in the car. "Look this over and tell me if there's anything on it you're not supposed to do."

V-crunches, planks, hip lifts, sit-ups, side crunches, bicycle kicks. It all looked standard to me.

"Turn it over."

My eyes opened wide when I looked at the other side.

"Too much?"

"Um...no."

"You're sure?"

It was way too much, but I'd never admit it. Even if it landed me back in the hospital.

"That's enough for today," Mantis said ninety minutes later.

He'd pushed me, but not as far as I originally thought he would.

Mantis put his hand on my shoulder and squeezed. "You won't get cleared if you let yourself get another injury on top of what you're already dealing with."

"I know," I muttered, wishing my body was strong enough to do the kind of workouts I'd done before I got shot. "How about a run?" I asked.

"A short one."

"Right." I smiled and walked over to the treadmill.

I was two miles in when my back spasmed. I pulled the cord to shut off the machine and leaned over with my hands on my knees.

"You okay?" Mantis asked, stopping his treadmill.

"My back," I grunted through the pain.

"Come with me. Can you climb up on the table?" he asked, leading me over to an empty massage room.

I gingerly twisted until I was close enough that I could get my bottom on the table. Once there, I rolled to my side and then onto my stomach.

"Where's your scar?" he asked, raising the back of my shirt. "Okay," he murmured, putting it back down and laying his big hands across my waist and gently kneading my flesh.

"God, that feels good," I murmured after he worked my muscles a few more minutes.

"If I remember right, I learned this from you." He moved to my bottom, again kneading to loosen the tightness that had caused the spasm.

I felt light-headed. If only I could change position enough to close my legs before Mantis noticed the effect he was having on me.

He switched sides, his hands once again too close for comfort. I gasped when he made his way down my thigh and his fingers touched the inside of my leg. I held my breath, willing him to move, but praying he wouldn't. All too soon, his magical touch was working my calves, but that didn't lessen my body's response.

"Does that feel good?" he murmured and I almost orgasmed.

His hands moved to my feet. My weakness, and he knew it.

"Can you feel this?" he asked, shattering the shell of the warm cocoon I'd been blanketed in.

"No," I answered, stifling a cry. I knew he was tapping the bottom of my right foot, but I couldn't feel it.

Mantis moved up my body, running his hand as he went, until it rested on my shoulder.

"Soon you will. I promise."

We met back out front after we'd both showered and changed.

"What's next?" I asked.

"How about a drive?"

"Where?"

"Tilley Ponds? It's cold, but we don't have to get out of the car."

"Sounds perfect." We'd taken walks around the cluster of ponds that were filled with lily pads in the spring, and ice skated on them when they were frozen. However, it probably wouldn't be a good idea for me to try to ice skate.

"No skating, though." He winked and smiled.

Had he read my mind? If so, had he known what I was thinking when he had his hands all over my body?

As he drove, my eyes drifted closed, and not because I was sleepy. Those hands, the sound of his voice, the way he'd hummed as he kneaded my flesh, never realizing he did it—made me lose my damn mind with memories of all the times it hadn't ended with just a simple massage.

* * *

"Manon," he whispered. "Look at me, baby."

Could I even open my eyes? Mantis had just ravished my body again and again and again, bringing me to one mind-blowing orgasm after another.

As I lay there, trying to catch my breath, trying to put the fires out in all the cells of my body that felt like there were still fireworks going off inside of them, Mantis ran his fingers over every inch of me.

"Flygirl," he whispered, tickling my ear with the cool air of his breath. "Look at me."

I stretched from my fingers to my toes, sighed happily, and opened my eyes to look into his beautiful blue ones.

"What you do to me," I murmured with a smile I couldn't help. "God, I feel so good."

His finger drew a circle around my nipple, bringing it back to a hardened nub and making me moan.

"So good? Is that what you said?"

"Mm-hmm."

"What about loved, Manon? Do you feel loved?"

I put my hand on his and looked into his eyes. "I do."

"That's good," he murmured, bringing his tongue to my nipple where his fingers still teased. "Because I love you, Manon—with all my heart, my fingers, my lips, my tongue, all of my body, but most importantly—with my soul." He parted my legs with his knee and with a quick thrust, we became one.

"I love you, Mantis," I said, arching my back, feeling him go deeper, like he was in my soul too.

* * *

"Where'd you go just now, baby?" he asked in a voice as soft and sweet and hot and fiery as the sex I'd been daydreaming about had always been between us. I opened my eyes, but didn't look at him. I couldn't, not without him knowing exactly what I'd been thinking about and how much I wanted to be with him like that—right this minute.

25

Dutch

"You'll be meeting with Mohamed Abdullahi," said Doc.

I recognized the name. The current president of Somalia, known as "Hermeja," had immigrated to the States and had worked as a civil servant in Upstate New York. He'd earned degrees in history and political science, all the while determined to one day return to his homeland. Some said he purchased his victory as president, funded by "organizations" anxious to further democracy in the small nation. Regardless, his anti-corruption platform resulted in a surprising win.

"Who else am I meeting with?"

"Ahmed Umar, the head of al-Shabaab."

I knew enough not to bother asking. There was no way Abdullahi and Umar would ever be in the same room at the same time.

"When do I leave?"

"Tomorrow. You'll have briefings in a few days at Ramstein before going on to Somalia."

The base in southwestern Germany served as head-quarters for the United States Air Force in Europe and also for NATO Allied Air Command, also known as AIRCOM. If I was stopping there, it meant that the war in Somalia had escalated enough that NATO was about to get involved.

I put my feet up on the coffee table that sat in front of the sofa in my hotel suite. I was up for the challenges of this op, probably the most important of my career. Like Mantis' mission in Afghanistan, when I got to the other side of it, no one would know it had even happened, and that was okay.

The politicians of the world could take credit for the things my K19 partners and I made happen all day long. I wasn't in it for the glory; I was in it to save the god-damn world.

Not everyone understood what drove men like me. There were probably a lot of people who believed I'd gone to the Air Force Academy because it was an easy road to a career. Nothing could've been further from the truth, both in why I'd done it and in its perceived ease. Nothing I'd done since the day I arrived in Colorado until where I found myself now, had been easy. Most of it had been gut-wrenchingly, heart-poundingly, soul-numbingly hard.

Like my grandfather and father before me, I'd been brought up knowing freedom wasn't free. The kind of life most took for granted was hard won, at the cost of hundreds and thousands of soldiers and their families who had given the ultimate sacrifice.

If I ever had a son or daughter, I'd want them to understand that it wasn't just their duty to serve their country; there was no greater honor.

I picked up the bottle of whiskey and glass that sat in front of me and poured my second shot of the night. As it burned all the way down my throat, I wondered where Mantis and Alegria were tonight.

Were they rediscovering all the things that made them fall in love with each other in the first place? I closed my eyes and imagined the two of them together. Sure, it hurt like hell, but at the same time, I felt a sense of honor in doing what I believed was the right thing, no matter what my own personal sacrifice might've been.

"Here's to you and the life I hope you build together," I said, raising my glass to the two imaginary friends standing in front of me. "I hope you both know how much I love you."

26

Mantis

The shower I took was ice-cold, not that it did any-thing to tame the erection I'd had since Alegria had climbed up on the massage table. It had gotten worse when I knew she was as affected by my hands on her as I was.

I held my gym bag in front of me as we walked to the car, but once we got inside, I didn't know what to do. Even in jeans, she'd be able to see the clear outline of how much I wanted her.

I closed my eyes and thought of the only thing that might tamp me down—Dutch.

The idea of betraying my friend squashed any thought I'd had of Alegria naked. I got in the car, repeat-ing Dutch's name in my head to the point where I was afraid I might say it out loud.

"Are you okay?"

"Fine. Why?"

"I don't know. You're moving weird. Did you hurt yourself too?"

"Nope," I said, looking out the driver's side window.

"I could always give you a massage when we get back to the house."

When I groaned, Alegria giggled. She was teasing me.

"I'll get you back for that, Flygirl."

She just laughed.

"Where have you two been all afternoon?" my mother asked when we walked in the front door.

"Tilley Ponds and then down to East Shippan."

"Brr."

"We didn't get out of the car," Alegria told her.

"There they are," said my dad, coming up from the basement. "Ready for dinner?"

"We thought we'd go to Sonny's," said my mother.

"I love Sonny's," Alegria said, practically swooning.

"Let's go, then."

"Hang on, Kip. Maybe they need to shower and change or something."

"We're good," I told her, doing my best not to picture Alegria with the warm water of a shower trickling down her naked body.

"Yeah, we're good," she said too, looking straight at me.

Was I imagining the heat in her eyes because I wanted to see it there so badly, or was she having the same thoughts I was?

"Have you heard from Dutch?" I asked her on our way to the restaurant.

"I was going to ask you the same thing."

"I haven't," I said and then looked away. Was it because he was traveling and couldn't get in touch, or was it because he was intentionally staying quiet?

"I left a message and sent a text," she murmured.

"We can check with Doc."

Alegria nodded.

"I was thinking we could fly tomorrow."

She turned her body toward mine. "Is the plane still here?"

"Why wouldn't it be?"

"Right. Maybe we should ask Doc when he wants it back on the West Coast."

I already had, and the answer Doc gave still perplexed me. He told me that the plane would stay in Westchester as long as I needed it. If I owned a two-million-dollar jet as nice as the SF50, I wouldn't want it out of my sight.

"As long as it's here…"

"We'll work through some maneuvers."

"What do you mean?" she asked.

"Off the books."

"Mantis…"

"The SF50 has yaw stability augmentation built into the flight control system. We can override it by using the rudder pedals, but it shouldn't be necessary."

"And if it is, you can take over."

I nodded. "That's right."

"Okay."

I wished she sounded excited rather than trepidatious. Maybe being on the controls tomorrow would help her attitude.

Since it was snowing, my dad pulled up to the front entrance of the restaurant to let my mother and Alegria out. I volunteered to walk in with him.

"We'll order appetizers, Kip," my mother said before she closed the car door behind her.

"I wonder where she thinks I'll have to park," said my father, circling the parking lot, looking for an empty spot. "Here we go," he said when he saw someone backing out.

"What did you want to talk to me about?" my dad asked as we climbed out of the car.

"Dutch."

27

Alegria

"I'm famished," said Minnie when we were seated at our table. "What sounds good?"

I laughed. "Everything. I've missed this place."

Minnie set her menu on the table. "Is that all you've missed?"

"That isn't fair," I murmured. "It was his choice."

"Biggest mistake of his life."

"I don't disagree, but it doesn't change the fact that he made it, and now we both have to live with it."

"What if he's changed his mind?" Minnie asked.

"Would it make a difference?"

When Mantis approached the table with his father and sat next to me, his knee brushed against mine, sending a jolt of electricity coursing through my body.

I moved my chair but giggled when he did too. "You're incorrigible."

"I am that."

"He takes after his father," said Minnie, winking.

When Kip put his arm around Minnie's shoulders and leaned in to kiss her cheek, I was reminded how

Mantis and I used to have the same easy affection. Dutch tried, but it just wasn't the same. My eyes met Mantis', and he winked like his mother had.

I closed my lids momentarily, wishing I could wipe away the memory of how we used to be together.

When he rested his palm on my knee, I thought about brushing it away, but the comfort of having it there felt too good. Instead, I put my hand on top of his. Too soon, the warmth of his touch was gone, and in its place, a chill spread throughout my body.

Willing him to put his hand back wasn't going to work any better than sitting there, wishing he'd tell me he'd made a terrible mistake or beg me to forgive him.

He wouldn't do any of those things in front of his parents, except maybe put his hand back on my leg, but he didn't do that either.

"Did I hear you say you're flying tomorrow?" Kip asked.

"That's the plan."

He pointed toward the window. "Better check flight conditions before you head to the airfield. It doesn't look good."

I followed Kip's gaze and saw it looked like a blizzard had started since we'd come inside.

"Maybe we should get our order to go," suggested Minnie.

Judging by how quickly the snow was falling, I agreed. Looking around the restaurant, many of the other diners had the same idea.

"I don't remember seeing this weather in the forecast," said Kip.

If I were cleared to fly, I would have been keeping track of changes in weather every fifteen minutes, but since I'd been grounded, I got out of the habit.

What other skills had I let lapse in the time since I was shot? When I finally got medical clearance, I'd be weeks behind where I'd been, rusty, and out of tune, like a guitar. Was it even worth trying, or was it time I gave up flying altogether?

"What do you think of that idea, Alegria?" I heard Minnie ask. I'd been lost in thought and hadn't realized anyone was talking to me.

"I'm sorry. What was the question?" I looked first at Minnie, then at Kip, and finally at Mantis.

"My mother asked if you'd like to leave now or wait for the food," he murmured. He had his elbow on the table and was running his finger back and forth over his lips while he waited for my answer.

"Whatever you think is best." I tried not to look at Mantis any more than I had to. It was like he was reading my mind and didn't like what he saw in it.

"Mrs. Cassman, Chef will have your food ready in about five minutes," said the waiter. "Sir," he said, addressing Kip, "you might want to bring the car to the door."

"I'll handle it," answered Mantis, holding out his hand for his father's keys.

"I'll come with you," I offered.

Mantis put his hand on my shoulder when I went to stand, and leaned down. "I can't risk you getting hurt, Flygirl," he whispered.

I felt the heat spread from somewhere in my torso, up my neck, and to my cheeks; I nodded in agreement. If this was the way I felt after being with Mantis less than twenty-four hours, how would I feel after we'd spent days together?

Mantis pulled the car up, but moved to the back seat so his father could drive us home.

I wanted to lean over and put my head on his shoulder or take his hand. But I couldn't. Not until I ended things with Dutch. As soon as I was able to speak with him privately, I had to tell him things were over between us. The feelings I had for Mantis were far too strong to do anything else.

Kip drove cautiously on the slow and treacherous drive back to the house. Based on the number of cars on the road, we hadn't been the only ones unprepared for the quick and drastic change in weather.

"Slow down, you bastards," I heard Kip mutter at the other drivers.

"Kip! Look out!" Minnie screamed moments later, right before a car careened into the side of ours, making impact right near the back-passenger door where I was sitting.

28

Mantis

I paced back and forth in the waiting room, hoping the next person who walked out of the double doors would have news.

My father had gone to see if he could find coffee, and my mother was sitting near the window. She'd been shaken up by the car's impact and had seen a doctor in the emergency room, but outside of a few bruises, she had no apparent signs of injury.

"You should go home," I told them when my father returned to the waiting room. I'd ridden in the ambulance with Alegria and had no idea how they'd even gotten to the hospital. My dad's car wasn't drivable. "I guess you don't have a car."

"Larry and his son brought us here and left the truck. It has chains and a plow, so if it gets worse, we'll still be able to get home."

I tried again to convince them to go get some rest, but they insisted they were staying, especially when the doctor came out and said Alegria was being taken directly into emergency surgery.

When the nurse came out at the next one-hour interval, she told me that the surgeons were getting ready to close. "I'll need you to sign this," she said, handing me a clipboard.

"What is it?"

"I need your signature as her medical power of attorney."

I hadn't considered that I'd still be listed as such. Why hadn't she changed it to either Dutch or Doc? It was something we'd have to discuss later. Maybe she'd forgotten.

"Hey, Doc," I said when he answered my call.

"I'm trying to reach Dutch. No luck yet."

"Thanks for the update. If you do talk to him, could you ask him if he's coming back?"

Doc didn't answer right away, but I could hear his wife asking a question in the background.

"What did Merrigan say?" I asked.

"How bad is it? Do I need to pull him from this op before he leaves for Mogadishu?"

If I were Alegria's boyfriend, and Dutch just our friend, I would've said there was no reason for him to abandon the op. But given our roles were reversed, I wasn't sure what to say. "I guess I won't be able to answer that until she's out of surgery."

"Roger that."

"Maybe just tell him Alegria's injuries are serious enough to warrant surgery, and it's his decision whether he flies back."

"What about her parents?"

I hadn't decided whether to contact them now or wait until I knew more.

I checked the time. It was after eleven, which meant it was four in the morning in Marseille, where they lived.

"I'll wait until she's out of surgery, and then I'll call them."

"I feel like this is my fault," my mother said when I put my phone back in my pocket.

"Why?"

"I'm the one who insisted we go out for dinner. If we'd just stayed home…"

I walked over, sat down next to her, and rubbed her shoulder. "You know better than to think that way, Mom. It doesn't do any good or change anything."

I looked up when someone came through the double doors, and recognized the charge nurse who had come out an hour earlier.

"Miss Mondreau is still in surgery," she said. "They were ready to close but then found more damage than they expected in the L1 to L5 area."

"She's recovering from a gunshot wound and subsequent surgery. I informed your team of that before she was taken in."

The woman put her hand on my arm. "We were aware, Mr. Cassman. What I'm saying is, there's more damage in that particular area than we expected."

I studied her when she repeated herself. "Are you saying there's something that was missed in her previous surgery?"

"No, I'm not saying that."

I waited for her to continue, but she didn't, which told me I was on the right track.

"I need to get back." She looked at her watch. "I'll see you in an hour with another update."

"Wait," I said when she started to walk away. "Is the damage something that could cause plantar neuropathy?"

She nodded. "Possibly."

"What did she say?" my mom asked when the nurse left the waiting room.

"They may have found something that would explain why her previous recovery wasn't going as well as it could've been."

"Is that a good thing?"

"I think so."

"Miss Mondreau is in the recovery room, but she's asking for someone named Mantis. Is that you?" a different nurse asked another hour later.

"That's me."

"You can see her now. Follow me."

"Can you give me an update on her condition?"

"Didn't the doctor come and talk to you?"

I shook my head.

"Wait here, then. I'll go get him."

She wasn't gone five minutes when the doctor came out the double doors.

"Mr. Cassman?"

I walked over to where the man stood. "How is she?"

"It was rough going initially. She reinjured her vertebrae before it had healed. On the other hand, we were able to remove bullet fragments that may have been giving her pain."

"Could the fragments also cause neuropathy?" I asked him like I'd asked the nurse.

"Potentially."

I followed the doctor to the recovery room. Seeing her on a gurney for the second time in only a few weeks shook me. The strongest woman I'd ever known looked weak and broken, something she wasn't any more used to than I was.

"Hey, Flygirl," I whispered, running my fingers through her hair.

She groaned and opened her lids. "Again?" she asked, her eyes darting around the room. "What happened? I feel like I've been run over by a truck."

"We got sideswiped by another car."

"I remember." Her eyes opened wide. "Your parents?"

"Out in the waiting room. They're both fine."

She closed her eyes.

"Get some rest, *mon coeur*. I'll be right here."

I watched her try to shift positions and then give up. "Can I help? Are you uncomfortable?"

"Mantis?"

"Yeah, sweetheart?"

"I can't move my legs."

I looked over at the nurse, who was typing into a computer. She got up when Alegria spoke and picked up a phone.

A couple of minutes later, the doctor who had spoken to me earlier stood by her bedside and rested his hand on her arm. "How are you doing, Miss Mondreau?"

"She can't move her legs," I told him.

He nodded and moved the sheet covering the lower half of her body. "It could be the effects of the anesthesia. You did have an epidural. Let's see how you feel in another hour."

I brushed Alegria's hair from her forehead.

After telling us he'd check back in, the doctor left and a different nurse came to take Alegria's vitals. "We're getting a room ready for her now," she said.

"Do you want me to ask Dutch to come back?"

Alegria shook her head.

"What about your parents?"

"No," she murmured.

"Sir, you'll have to step out for a moment," said yet another nurse.

Alegria opened her eyes and reached for my hand. "Don't go," she whispered.

"I'll be right outside. As soon as they'll let me, I'll come back in."

"No!" she pleaded, this time clutching my hand.

"It's okay," the nurse murmured. "You can stay."

Once Alegria was in a regular room on the surgical floor and had fallen asleep, I stepped outside the door and called Dutch. It went straight to voicemail. My next call was to Doc.

"It's probably just the epidural," I said. "Although the doctor seemed surprised that she couldn't move her legs."

"Is there anything we can do?" Doc asked.

"I'm not sure how to handle this."

"Meaning?"

I shook my head. "I don't know. For now, I'll stay with her."

"How is she?" asked my mom, walking up just as I ended the call with Doc.

"Sore, groggy..."

"What aren't you saying, son?" asked my dad.

"I'm sure it's nothing. I should get back in there in case she wakes up." I hugged both of my parents. "You should head home. I'll let you know more later. I…uh… she doesn't want me to leave."

"We'll bring you a change of clothes when we come back," my mom said before turning to my dad. "Kip, why don't you pull the truck up while I talk to Gehring."

My father looked confused, but only momentarily. Once he was gone, my mother looped her arm through mine.

"Okay, it's just you and me. Tell me what's really going on."

"Alegria can't move her legs."

29

Alegria

Every time I closed my eyes, I flashed back to the moment right before the crash. Was the universe punishing me for my decision to end things with Dutch? Mantis had asked if I wanted Dutch called back from the op, but I didn't. It was Mantis I wanted with me—so much I couldn't stand the idea of him leaving my side.

I could hear him outside of the room, talking to his parents, but not clearly enough that I could follow their conversation.

"You're awake," he said, poking his head around the corner of the doorway.

I nodded, wishing he was close enough that I could feel the comfort of his touch.

"Hi, sweetheart," said his mom, walking in before him. She leaned down and kissed my forehead. "Can I do anything for you?"

I shook my head. "No, but thanks."

"Kip and I will be back later. If you change your mind, Gehring can call us."

When his mother left, Mantis pulled a chair closer to the bed, sat down, and held my hand.

"Don't leave," I said again.

"I'm not goin' anywhere, Flygirl."

"My head hurts."

"Do you want me to call for the nurse?"

"No."

"Does this help?" he asked, running his fingers through my hair.

"It does," I whispered, tears spilling from my eyes.

"Don't cry, *mon coeur*. You're going to feel better after you get some more rest."

Something was telling me Mantis was wrong.

30

Dutch

My phone blew up when I turned it on after the plane I was on landed in Germany. I'd missed several calls, had messages waiting, and texts marked urgent from Mantis and Doc.

I waited until I was outside of the airport in a transportation waiting area where I had some privacy before I read the texts.

I read Doc's first. *There's been an accident.*

I scrubbed my face with my hand, fearing the worst and not wanting to confirm it.

Before I could respond, something heavy hit my head, and everything went black. The phone I'd been holding in my hand now lay by the side of the road.

31

Mantis

Every time Alegria tried to move, I woke up. "Any better?" I'd ask, hoping the effects of the epidural were wearing off.

Each time she'd answer the same way, "Nothing has changed."

I checked my phone, hoping there was word from either Dutch or Doc, but there wasn't. Soon, the doctor should be in, and maybe we'd get a better idea why she still couldn't move her legs.

"Good morning," I said when she opened her eyes and met my gaze. I brushed the hair from her forehead like I had so many times in the last few hours. I couldn't explain it, but it was as though I had to have some part of my body touching hers at all times. "Are you hungry?"

She shook her head. "Not really. You can get something to eat, though."

I looked at my phone again. It was almost eight. Not that I'd leave her anyway, but I wouldn't risk even a quick trip to the cafeteria knowing I might miss the doctor.

"Good morning," said my mother, walking into the room with something that smelled so good it made my stomach growl.

"What's in there?" I asked, reaching for the bag.

She swatted my hand. "Something for Alegria."

Alegria smiled when my mom handed the bag to her. It was a beautiful sight to see. I couldn't remember if she'd smiled at all since the surgery.

"Warm croissants. Yum," she murmured.

"There's raspberry jam in the bottom of the bag too."

I was starving, but the idea that my mother had found something Alegria wanted to eat kept me from asking her to share.

"Why don't you take a break," my mom suggested. "I'll stay with Alegria."

I shook my head. "I don't want to miss the doctor." When neither she nor Alegria appeared to have heard me, I stood and went into the hallway.

"Mantis," said Doc, answering my call on the first ring.

"I just realized how early it is out there."

"Early? Zero six hundred?" Doc laughed. "Laird makes sure we don't sleep past sunrise."

"Right." I had no desire to talk about Doc and Merrigan's baby. I wanted answers.

"Where the hell is Dutch?"

"I wish I knew. Still no response."

"Are you worried?"

"Not yet. It isn't like he hasn't pulled this shit before."

I nodded, even though Doc couldn't see me do it. This wasn't the first time Dutch had gone dark during prep for an op. The fact that he was doing it after Doc had left messages that Alegria had been in an accident, pissed me the hell off.

"Let me know when you hear from him."

"Are you okay?" my mother asked, stepping into the hallway where I stood shaking my head and staring at my phone.

"Yeah. I'd be better if Dutch would return my phone calls."

"There may be a reason he isn't."

I looked up. "What are you talking about?"

"Come with me," she said, putting her arm through mine.

I shook free. "I can't leave right now. I don't want to miss hearing what the doctor has to say."

"Okay, I'll tell you here, but keep your voice down." My mother grasped my arm for a second time. "He's doing it on purpose."

"Mom," I sighed. "I can't do this right now."

"Dutch wants the two of you to figure things out, and he doesn't think you can do it with him in the middle. He must've sensed you'd invite her to come home with you and that she'd agree."

"I'm sorry, but there's no way he 'sensed' anything."

"Maybe he knows you both better than you think."

"Bottom line this for me. What you're saying is he's intentionally not responding?"

"I believe so."

"Alegria was in a car accident, had emergency surgery, and can't move her legs, but he's playing games. Fuck him."

"Gehring—"

"No, Mom. This is bullshit."

I saw the doctor walking past the nurses' station and went back into Alegria's room. It was clear by the look on her face that she'd heard at least part of our conversation.

"There's nothing in the MRI or CT scan that would explain the paralysis, and at this point, I'm hesitant to open you up again until you've had a chance to heal."

Alegria turned her head and looked out the window. The doctor didn't seem fazed by her lack of response.

"In the meantime, we're hopeful that things will progress as they should and the paralysis either goes away completely or, at the very least, diminishes."

"Thank you," I said, since Alegria had stopped communicating or even acknowledging the man was in the room.

"I'll check back later in the day," he said before walking back out to the hallway.

"Talk to me, Flygirl."

"What were you saying about Dutch?"

"Neither Doc nor I have been able to reach him."

"From what I could overhear, Dutch is staying away intentionally. Is that right?"

"In theory." I reached over to touch her face, and she moved away. "What's going on?"

"My parents are arriving this afternoon."

"Your parents? I didn't realize—"

"That I am capable of using a phone?"

I shook my head. This was hardly the first time I'd seen Alegria in bitch mode, and right now, she had every right to act any way she wanted to. I'd learned long ago to walk away when she got like this, but that wasn't something I could do now. "Try to get some rest," I murmured.

"I don't want to rest," she snapped. "All I've done is sleep."

"It's what your body needs to heal."

By the look on her face, I knew every word I said was only making things worse.

"Tell you what, maybe I'll head home for a little while and let you have some time to yourself."

I couldn't tell whether the idea of me leaving made her happy or sad.

"Fine."

"You know how to reach me if you need anything."

"Right."

I leaned down, put my arm around her shoulders so she couldn't jerk away again, and kissed the top of her head.

"Happy New Year," I whispered.

32

Alegria

Once I was certain Mantis was gone, I turned the upper half of my body toward the window, clutched the pillow to my chest, and let the tears flow that I'd held in since I overheard Mantis' conversation with his mother.

I hadn't realized what day it was, but then, I had no reason to celebrate.

This New Year's Eve wasn't going to be much different than the two before it. Last year I didn't have any idea where in the world Mantis was, or even if he was still alive. The year before, we'd had a terrible fight, and he'd left, much like he did today.

I'd done a lot of thinking while I lay in yet another hospital bed with my body broken.

My life as I'd known it was over, and it was time to make some drastic changes. Once my parents arrived, they'd help me figure out my next best course of action. Whatever that turned out to be, my new life had to be vastly different than the one I'd been trying so hard to get back to.

Only yesterday I'd begged Mantis not to leave me. Then, I'd still believed the paralysis in my legs would go away when the epidural wore off. The fact that it hadn't, was what made me decide it was time to move forward and leave the past behind, particularly the part with Mantis and Dutch in it. A new year meant a new life.

I closed my eyes against the other memories I had of New Year's Eves, the ones that had been good between Mantis and me.

* * *

"Where are we going?" I asked.

"Be patient and have faith."

"You know I don't like surprises."

Mantis laughed. "You don't like feeling out of control. You love surprises."

Was that true? I thought back on all the times he'd insisted, like he was now, that I be patient and have faith in him.

"It's good for you to let go every now and then."

I rested my head against the seat and fought the anxiety that came along with not knowing where we were going or what we were doing. Within minutes, I dozed off. Each time my head bobbed to my chest, I'd wake up.

"You can't even let go and sleep." He laughed.

"Shut up," I muttered, irritated he was finding so much humor in my shortcomings.

Mantis put his hand on my thigh and squeezed my bare flesh. "I promise you're gonna love this."

His fingers made their way closer to my sex, and I felt the muscles in my body, one by one, release tension. My eyes half closed, but not because I was sleepy. Instead, my nerve-endings were on high alert, willing his fingers to dip under the edge of my skirt. I pouted when he pulled his hand away entirely.

"Make no mistake, I plan to pick up where we left off very soon," he said when I groaned at his fingers' absence.

"How soon?"

He turned his head and smiled. He was right about my inability to give up control. The only time I did it willingly was when Mantis had his hands on my naked body. Then I gave in enthusiastically.

"I can't keep my hands off of you," he murmured, running his fingers up my thigh like I'd wanted him to moments ago. "Lift your skirt."

I did.

"Show me what you want me to do to you."

His hand moved from my thigh to my breast.

"Show me," he said again, this time pinching my left nipple with his deft fingers, the ones that made me beg, and plead, and even scream.

"Please, Alegria," he murmured.

When his grasp tightened on my nipple, I put my hand on my own flesh. In seconds, he grabbed my wrist and brought my fingers to his mouth, licking away every trace of my essence.

"Do you know how much I want you?" he asked.

With my skin flushed and a terrible ache between my legs, I wanted him just as much.

* * *

I shuddered, remembering the magical hold he had on my body then, and every other time we'd made love.

It wasn't a surprise that Dutch had never been able to bring me to the heights of pleasure that Mantis did. He was far too tentative, waiting for me to control the situation like I did with everything else. There were a handful of times when he showed signs of taking over, but when he'd backed off, I was left disappointed to the point of no longer being interested.

I tried to squeeze my thighs together to assuage the ache that came whenever I thought about Mantis' hands or mouth on me, but my legs wouldn't cooperate.

If only we'd made love one last time, I could've held the memory of it forever.

As it was, I had to reach much further back to relive the last time he'd brought me to the precipice and then sent me hurling into the abyss of ecstasy.

33

Mantis

I didn't feel like talking when my father picked me up at the hospital, and thankfully, it was something he'd always recognized easily.

"Your mother went shopping," he said when we pulled into the driveway.

"I'm going to need to rent a car."

My dad nodded. "Let me know if there's anything I can do to help." He paused. "You know, like drive you to the rental place."

"Right."

My father squeezed my shoulder. "How about a beer?"

"Isn't it the middle of the morning?"

"Sure is, but by the look of you, you need one."

"I think something stronger is in order."

"Done."

I followed my dad into the house. "Maybe I should go get the car before we open any bottles."

"Good thinking."

"What's up with you?" I asked him. As much as I didn't want to talk about Alegria or Dutch or even K19, my father's behavior warranted a conversation.

"I've decided to retire."

"Oh. Uh, do you still work?"

My dad had run a successful manufacturing consultancy for many years, and for the most part, worked from home.

"Maybe not as much as I used to, but enough that I think about it, and I don't want to think about work anymore."

"You'd rather start drinking first thing in the morning?"

He smiled. "I don't intend to drink any more often than I do now. However, today, you look like you need to tie one on tight."

"I don't want to talk about it."

"Who said anything about talking?"

An hour later, we hadn't gone to get a rental car; I hadn't even reserved one. What I had done, though, was tell my father every detail about what had gone down between Alegria and me, and Alegria and Dutch. I couldn't talk about the latter in detail, but I could convey my anger at what my supposed best friend had done.

My dad hadn't said much, nor had he had much to drink. When I stopped after the first round of whiskey, my dad had too. "She did cut you loose," my father said when I finally shut up enough that the man could get a word in.

I shrugged. "I like to think of it as a mutually agreed upon decision."

My father laughed out loud. "What a load of bullshit. You refused to do as she asked, and she dumped you."

"You're right."

I was six feet three inches tall and weighed two hundred and thirty pounds, yet my father still bested me in both. When Kip Cassman rested his hand on a man's shoulder and squeezed, like he'd just done to me, whoever it was would feel it down to their toes.

"How's Jonas?" I asked, pushing the memory of how my oldest brother and I had always worked out with our father, but our younger brother never joined us.

"He's good. Theresa just had that sweet baby girl, Alana. I always wanted a girl, but I guess I was just meant to be a grandpa to a couple. No offense to you or your brothers."

I cringed at my father's use of the plural word. I no longer had brothers; now I only had one. "None taken."

"What in the world?" said my mother, coming in from the garage to find us both with our feet up on her coffee table.

"Just a little father-son bonding, Minnie."

She walked over and picked up my father's glass. "Whiskey? At ten in the morning?"

"I think we started closer to nine."

She threw her hands up in the air and stomped off to the kitchen. "Is this your second bottle?" she hollered.

"No. Why?" I asked.

She came back in, gripping the bottle's neck. "You've hardly had any."

I watched as my father stood, walked over to my mom, took the whiskey from her hand, and then leaned down and kissed her.

"You used to like the taste of whiskey on my lips," he said when she pulled away.

That was my cue to leave. It was bad enough that I'd just had my heart stomped on; I didn't need to see evidence of how a relationship was supposed to work from my parents.

I went out the back door instead of the front. I hadn't been in the yard behind my parents' house yet, and I knew that, sooner or later, I'd have to.

The tree we'd planted seventeen years ago, in Ian's memory, was easily over forty feet tall. Two Adirondack chairs sat beneath it, where I knew my parents sat and talked about their firstborn.

Even right after it happened, they hadn't shied away from talking about their feelings. At the time, I was thirteen years old, Jonas only ten.

"It's okay to cry," our father had told us. "We miss him, and we're sad that he's gone."

I hadn't cried then; I'd gotten angry. I was still angry, and probably would be for the rest of my life.

It didn't matter that I'd personally snuffed the life out of Bagish Safi's body. Nothing would ever bring my brother back or assuage the rage inside of me whenever I thought about the day the two planes hit the World Trade Center.

The rage drove me then, and it still did. I'd vowed that day to become a fighter pilot so I could shoot any plane out of the sky that threatened to bring harm to the United States and to families like mine.

I stood beneath the tree, rubbing my chest. It wasn't that the ache of missing my brother was so strong I needed to rub it away; it was that the rage wasn't as strong as it used to be, and that worried me.

I couldn't allow my anger or determination to avenge my brother's death to diminish. If I did, I'd no longer be honoring Ian's memory.

I felt my father's hand on my shoulder. This time he didn't squeeze; he just rested it there.

"Have a seat," he said, motioning to one of the snow-covered chairs. I brushed the snow away like my father did and sat down.

"I see the war waging inside of you, son," he began. "Maybe it's time to surrender your arms."

I shook my head. "I can't."

"Nothing you do, no one you kill, will bring him back."

I looked into my father's eyes. I hadn't told him about the last time I was in Afghanistan, about the mission, or its outcome. I understood what he was saying, though.

When I'd watched the last man die who I held responsible for my brother's death, I didn't feel avenged; I felt empty.

While I'd put one foot in front of the other, I did so without the same sense of purpose I had only hours before. I'd struggled to bring that feeling back—the one of certainty in the mission, certainty in my life's work—but it wasn't there anymore.

I navigated my way through the days that followed, unable to decide what I should do next. Finally, I'd returned to the States.

All I'd thought about on my way back was Alegria, and how maybe, just maybe, I'd reached the place in my life where I could let go of revenge and just live. But it had been too late. Not only was she with Dutch, she was done with me. She'd made that perfectly clear then and earlier today when she'd dismissed me.

The glimmer of hope I'd had twenty-four hours before was gone, and in its wake, I found myself a man without a mission and without love in my life.

"Don't give up on her," my father murmured.

"How did you know I was thinking about Alegria?"

He shrugged. "What else would you be thinking about?"

"She doesn't want me anymore."

My father shook his head. "You're wrong."

"You weren't there this morning. She went from begging me not to leave her side to practically booting me out of the room."

It was a long time before my dad spoke again. "Put yourself in her position," he said finally. "Would you allow yourself to lean on her?"

"I did. I was in her position. She helped me get my medical clearance."

"And what if you hadn't been able to get it, no matter how hard you worked? What then?"

"It wouldn't have changed things between us."

His gaze was penetrating. "Don't lie to yourself."

"What are you saying, that I would've ended our relationship because I couldn't fly?"

I waited, but my dad didn't answer. The longer I remained silent, the more I knew he was right. If I'd never been able to fly again, I couldn't have stayed with her. I wasn't sure I could've stayed in the Air Force.

"You're running on empty. Get some rest and then go back and see her."

I nodded. I hadn't slept more than a few minutes at a time last night, and not at all the night before. Maybe after I got some rest, I'd be able to figure out how to convince her I wanted back in her life, and this time, for good.

Of course that meant she'd have to end things with Dutch. Was that something I could ask of her? Could I do that to Dutch?

34

Alegria

"I don't recommend moving her yet," the doctor told my parents, but they refused to compromise.

"Before she entered this hospital she could walk," my father bellowed. "Now she cannot."

They were proposing I be moved from Stamford Hospital to the Spaulding Rehabilitation Hospital in Boston. The doctors there specialized in neuromuscular disorders and were purported to be the best in treating those who had suffered brain or spinal injuries resulting in paralysis.

"Boston is over three hours from Stamford. Your daughter is not stable enough to make that long of a trip."

My father waved his hand in the air. "I have arranged for medical transport via helicopter."

The doctor shook his head. "I still advise against this."

My papa was relentless in his determination, not just in this case, but in all things. I knew there would be no talking him out of it, regardless of whether I was well enough to be moved or not.

"I don't want to transfer to a different hospital."

"Manon," my mother began. "Please do as your father asks."

I closed my eyes and wished Mantis were here to take my side against my parents. Why had I pushed him away again when all I wanted was for him to be with me?

35

Dutch

I nuzzled the neck of the sweet-smelling body I spooned, grounding my hardness between the soft cheeks of her bottom—and my eyes flew open.

I moved away from the sleeping form and sat up, looking around. I had no idea where I was or who the naked woman in bed next to me was.

She groaned and rolled over in her sleep.

"What's your name?" I asked, trying not to frighten the doe-eyed girl.

"Gretchen," she answered, clutching the sheet to her naked body.

"No offense, Gretchen, but what happened last night?"

"Last night?"

"Did I have a lot to drink?"

She shook her head, but I sensed she wasn't answering me; she didn't understand what I was asking.

"Drunk. Was I drunk?" I didn't feel hungover, I felt like I'd entered an alternate universe—one in which I couldn't remember where I was or even my own name.

Before she could respond, the hotel room door opened. I spun around to give housekeeping a piece of my mind for entering without knocking, but instead of a hotel maid, someone else I didn't recognize stood in the doorway.

"Who the hell are you?"

"Your worst fucking nightmare," answered the man dressed like a damn al-Qaeda terrorist.

36

Mantis

"I don't understand," I said for the third time to the nurse who continued to insist Manon Mondreau was no longer a patient in their hospital. "She couldn't have just gotten up and walked out." I cringed at the flippant remark. No, she couldn't have, because she was paralyzed from the waist down, but that wasn't what I meant.

"Mr. Cassman," said a familiar voice.

I spun around to face the doctor I'd seen several hours earlier.

"Where is she?"

"HIPPA prevents me from divulging that information."

"No. It doesn't. I'm her medical power of attorney. Check her chart."

"Her power of attorney was changed."

"What are you talking about?"

"You are no longer listed."

"Who is?"

The doctor glared at me and folded his arms. "I can't answer that."

I stomped off and then turned around and came back. "Were her parents here?"

"There's nothing more I can tell you," the doctor responded, walking away.

I didn't bother following him. Instead, I called Doc. "I'm at Stamford Hospital and Alegria is not. They won't tell me anything other than she's no longer a patient. I need to find her."

"Roger that," Doc said without asking any questions.

"Can you help me?"

"Of course. I'll get back to you as soon as I can."

"Any word on Dutch?"

"Negative."

I called Alegria, but when my call went straight to voicemail, I wasn't surprised.

I thought about calling her parents, but wasn't sure I even had their numbers. I'd told Doc that I'd call them about Alegria's condition, but at the time, I hadn't been thinking about whether I had their contact information.

Over the years, they'd made no secret that they didn't approve of my relationship with their daughter.

The year I'd surprised Alegria by taking her to France to celebrate the new year, I was anxious to meet them. At the time, I'd wondered why she hadn't spent Christmas with them since she enrolled at the Air Force Academy. After we arrived in Paris, I understood why not.

* * *

"My family isn't big on holidays," she explained when I asked why she was hesitant to let them know she was there.

"That's okay, not everyone is. You still want to see them though, don't you?"

She shrugged. "Sure I do, but…"

"But, what?"

"It might be better if I went alone. Just the first time. You know, to prepare them."

"Prepare them for me?" Was she kidding? I'd just surprised her with a trip to France, and she had to *prepare* her parents to meet me?

There'd never been an instance when the parents of whomever I was dating hadn't like me. Hell, most of the time, they were ready to have me sign on the dotted line that I'd marry their daughter one day.

"It's just that…"

"Say it, Manon."

"They aren't overly fond of…Americans."

"And yet they let Americans provide your education. You became a United States citizen, and you are in the military, having vowed to protect *your* country from all sworn enemies, even France if it came to it."

"They weren't in favor of my attending the Air Force Academy."

"What did you say?"

"They didn't agree with my decision."

"And what? They disowned you?"

I never would've said it if I thought, even for a minute, that she would nod her head.

"You're kidding?"

"I'm not."

I pulled her into my arms. "I'm sorry."

"What for? You didn't do anything."

"I brought you here."

"I love Paris. I love that you brought me here."

* * *

We'd made the best of it, but we didn't see her parents while we were there. In fact, it was five more years before I even met them. And then, I wished I hadn't. They were overbearing and egotistical. They'd barely recognized me as a human being, let alone my presence in the room.

It shouldn't have been a surprise that they'd either moved her from Stamford or instructed the hospital staff to say they had, just to keep me away from her. In fact, the latter was the more likely scenario.

I was about to call Doc and tell him my theory, when a call came in from him instead.

"She's in Boston."

What the hell? "Where in Boston?"

"Spaulding Rehabilitation Hospital."

"You're sure?"

"Positive. She was flown by medical helicopter this morning, piloted by Pierre Mondreau, and accompanied by his wife, Matille."

"I forgot he was a pilot. Although I didn't know he was licensed to fly helicopters."

"Pierre flew with the Aviation *Légère de l'Armée de Terre* originally," said Doc.

The "land army," as the French military called it, was made up primarily of infantry; however, helicopters were considered part of that branch, but used mainly for medical evacuation.

I remembered Alegria telling me that Pierre's service in the French military was one of her father's primary objections to her choosing to transfer to the United States Air Force Academy and, ultimately, becoming an officer and citizen of the country. Although she'd also told me that her father was opposed to her serving in the French military too.

I ended the call and pulled up Spaulding Rehab's details on my phone. It made sense that they'd taken her there; it was second in the nation for spinal cord injuries resulting in paralysis.

I tried to call Alegria again, but like before, it went straight to voicemail.

37

Alegria

I looked out the window of my new hospital room and sighed. My father had been rude to every person we interacted with, and my mother wasn't much better. Did they really think berating the hospital staff would result in my receiving better care? The nurses probably hated me by now.

"Stop, *Maman, s'il vous plait,*" I begged, but my mother didn't act as though she'd heard me. Instead, she was looking at her phone.

"Where is my phone?" I asked.

My mother shrugged.

"You don't know? Is it with my other belongings?"

"I don't believe so."

"Would you please check?"

My mother stood and walked over to a closet. I couldn't see what was in it from where I was.

"I don't see it."

Had she even looked? "Please check again."

"I told you I don't see it," she said, closing the closet with more force than was necessary.

I felt equally angry and powerless. The idea that I may have this same struggle—unable to get up and check for myself—long term, made me want to hit something.

"You have no need for it anyway."

"What did you say?"

"You heard me. You have no need for your phone." My mother stood and walked out of the room.

What had I been thinking when I called my parents? Had I really believed that they would treat me any differently now than they had the rest of my life?

Rather than being sympathetic to my condition, it was as though they believed it was my fault I was paralyzed. They went as far as suggesting that if I hadn't been with Mantis and his family, I wouldn't have sustained further injuries. They didn't disparage just Mantis; they went after his parents too.

"It was an accident," I'd told them, to no avail.

They acted disgusted by the whole thing, as well as very put out by having to come to the States and deal with me.

To think that I'd mentioned to Dutch that if I'd been cleared to fly I would've gone "home" to France.

I'd actually told him that then I wouldn't be a burden to him. Maybe not to him, but I certainly would have been a burden to my parents. I always had been. The nannies with whom they'd left me weren't much better. They all saw me as a spoiled brat, when nothing could've been further from the truth. I was more feral than spoiled.

Years ago, when Mantis surprised me by taking me to Paris, I'd told him they'd disowned me when I left for America and the Air Force Academy. The truth was, they'd never had much more than a passing interest in me to begin with.

It was evident by where they lived and the life they led, that my family had a great deal of money—how much, I didn't know. Other than their gift of the apartment in New York City, I had been expected to earn my own way.

While my father had made arrangements for me to be flown to Boston via medical helicopter, it likely had far less to do with me than it did him and my mother. They would've been greatly inconvenienced if they'd had to make the four-hour drive.

I waited for my mother to come back into the room so I could ask her again about my phone, but after an hour passed, I assumed that my parents had gone to their hotel. It remained to be seen whether they came back tonight. I wasn't optimistic nor was I surprised that they'd left without saying goodbye.

I closed my eyes and thought about how hurt Mantis looked earlier when I'd shunned him. My treatment of him was no better than my parents' treatment of me. Why, knowing how much their behavior hurt me, did I find myself acting much like they did so often? One would think I'd do the exact opposite.

Now I didn't even have the means to call and apologize to Mantis or let him know where I was. Had someone at the other hospital told him I'd been moved? Did he know where?

I felt trapped, like I was a prisoner in this room and in my own body. If I willed Mantis to come and rescue me, would he? Or would he think I'd left so he wouldn't know where I was?

When I drifted to sleep, I didn't dream about Mantis. I dreamed of Dutch.

It was dark, and I could barely see. Why didn't I have a night-vision device with me? I looked down and saw that instead of clothing, I wore a hospital gown. I couldn't feel my feet, and when I bent farther to look at them, I saw I didn't have any. It was as though my legs had simply faded into nothing rather than ending in stumps where feet used to be.

"Dutch?" I called out into the darkness.

"Over here," he called back. "But keep your voice down."

I put my hands out in front of me and made my way in the direction of his voice.

"Don't come any closer," he warned. "They'll kill you."

"What about you? Won't they kill you too?"

"I'm already dead, Flygirl."

I woke with a cry when I felt a band tighten on my arm and tried to wrench it away.

"Whoa, whoa, whoa," said the nurse. "That's the blood pressure cuff." She loosened it, pulled a chair closer to the bed, and took my wrist in her hand. "Your pulse is racing," she said. "Take a few deep breaths and try to calm yourself down. You had a nightmare."

Was it a nightmare? It had felt so real.

When the nurse stood and brushed against my leg, I gasped.

"What?"

"*I felt that!*" I exclaimed. "I felt your hand on my leg."

She reached over me, turned on the overhead light, and moved the sheet and blanket so she could see my legs.

"Close your eyes," she said. "Can you feel that?"

I nodded. It was faint, but I could feel it.

"Where are my fingers?"

"On my left knee."

"What about now?"

"My ankle."

"Which one?"

"Left."

"How many fingers do you feel?"

I shook my head. "I can't tell."

"But you can feel the pressure?"

"That's right."

The nurse moved the bed covers back over my legs. "Do you want the light on or off?"

"On, please."

"I'll be back in a few minutes. I'm going to call the resident on duty."

Fifteen minutes passed before the nurse returned with the doctor. He examined my legs much the same way the nurse had, only this time, I could feel three fingers on my ankle.

"This is great news," he said, making notes on my chart on a laptop. "Dr. Gertman will be making rounds early tomorrow morning. He'll order whatever tests he determines appropriate then."

"Wait," I said when the nurse followed the doctor out of the room. "Is there a phone I can use? I need to make a call."

She pointed next to the bed. Only then did I realize that without my cell, I wouldn't have access to anyone's number. It wasn't like I routinely memorized them when they changed as often as we rotated burner phones.

"Do you have a cell phone? Maybe it's in here." The nurse looked in the same closet my mother had earlier. "I don't see one."

I rested my head against the pillow. I didn't want to admit to the nurse that my mother had probably taken it with her when she left earlier.

38

Mantis

I left five messages for Alegria before admitting what I'd known before I left the first one. She was refusing to talk to me, just like she'd refused when I came back from Afghanistan.

That we'd inched closer only to be so far away from each other again, hurt like hell. She'd needed me, and then suddenly she didn't anymore. It was as though she'd flipped the switch on and then back off again.

"Can I make you something to eat?" my mother asked, joining me in the kitchen.

It was only a little before dawn, and I wasn't hungry. I might not be hungry at all today. My mom pulled out one of the chairs at the kitchen table and sat down.

"Where did you say Alegria is?" she asked.

"At a rehab hospital in Boston."

"You had no idea she was being moved?"

I shook my head. "None whatsoever."

"Call her and ask."

"I have. It goes straight to voicemail."

"Go see her."

"What if she doesn't want to see me?"

The way my mother smiled made me feel like I was five years old again. "Why wouldn't she?"

I shrugged. "It wouldn't be the first time," I muttered.

She stood and started taking things out of the cupboard and refrigerator, amassing a pile on the kitchen counter.

"What are you doing?"

"Making cookies. Maybe brownies too."

"Why?"

She squeezed my shoulder when she walked past me to turn the oven on. "Your nieces and nephews will be ascending on our house one day soon."

Her smile at the thought warmed me all over. I still hadn't seen Jonas, Theresa, or their kids, and I was anxious to.

"When will they be here?"

"Let's see...I'm fuzzy on what day, but Jonas said nine, so Theresa is probably thinking more like ten. With four littles to wrangle—not that the baby takes much wrangling—my best guess is between eleven and noon. I feel better being prepared, whichever day it is."

I smiled. "You have it all figured out, don't you?"

"There was a time I had three littles of my own."

My mom was great about celebrating the happy memories of having three boys, but at times like these, early in the morning when the day was still raw, I saw the pain that sat so close to her surface.

"Ian was so much older than you and your brother, though. It wasn't as hard for me to do things as it is for Theresa, who has four under ten."

"Really? God, I've never thought of it in those terms."

"She manages fine, as does Jonas."

I shook my head and took another sip of coffee, closing my eyes and wishing Alegria was here with us, talking to my mother, helping her make cookies, and bestowing one of her smiles of understanding on me.

"Ethan is the same age Ian was when you were born. He's a big help to his mama, just like Ian was to me."

My older brother would've turned forty this year, and that made me feel my own age. Thirty—and without much of a sense of purpose anymore.

What might life have been like if Ian hadn't run into the second tower on that fateful morning eighteen years ago? Would he still be a firefighter? Would he be married, have kids like Jonas did, or be a bachelor like I was?

"Go see her, Gehring."

"I don't know, Mom. There has to come a time when I respect the fact that Alegria doesn't want me in her life."

"But she does."

"No offense, but how do you know what she wants?"

My mom sat back down at the table and put her hand on mine. "Tell me what you know about her. Five things. The five most important things."

"Wow. Um..."

"Take your time." She stood and went back to making cookies.

This was tough. I knew countless things about her, but naming only five, and what I considered the top five, was difficult.

She was as smart or smarter than any professor at the Air Force Academy, more beautiful than a super model, stubborn, prideful, independent, feisty, funny, and sexy as hell. She was warm and caring but could be as aloof and cold as the Arctic. She was demanding of others, but equally of herself.

And then there was the side of her that was insecure, doubtful of her worth in life, needy, clingy, and petulant.

"I don't know if I can narrow what I know about Alegria to five things."

"Think about her as Manon, then."

I smiled at my mother's insight. We all hid behind our call signs from time to time.

"That isn't much easier."

"It should be."

I decided to test the water. "Smart, stubborn, independent..."

"Keep going. Two more."

"Sexy as hell."

My mother looked around and smiled.

"You didn't tell me to edit."

"And I don't want you to. One more."

I thought for several minutes about what final word I would use to describe her, weighing all the things I'd thought of. "Insecure," I finally settled on.

"One would wonder what kind of wars wage inside of a woman like that."

I smiled. "Would one?"

She smiled too and nodded. "Think about it, Gehring."

I didn't need to. I understood what my mother was trying to get me to recognize.

"What's the worst that can happen if you go to Boston?" she asked.

"She could refuse to see me, rip my heart out, and leave me a shell of the man I once was."

"Hasn't she already done most of that?"

"Thanks, Mom."

"I'm serious, Gehring. Haven't you already experienced all of that and lived through it?"

"Doesn't mean I want to again."

"No? You're saying she isn't worth it?"

"Is that what I'm saying?"

"More than my other two sons, you're the one I've always believed would never give up. You'll fight for what you believe in until the bitter end, and then you'll fight again to keep it that way. Don't give up, Gehring. Keep fighting—not just for what you believe in—for the woman you love."

"What if I can't do both?"

She shook her head. "You can do both and pile another ten things on top of them, and you know it."

"You have such faith in me."

She moved her chair so she was facing me. "Yes, I have faith in you. I believe you are a superhero, my sweet son. Don the mask, or the cape, or however your superhero hides himself away from the world, and go out and do what needs to be done."

"What's going on in here?" My father walked into the kitchen, rubbing his eyes. "You both look so serious."

"Gehring was just telling me that he's leaving for Boston later this morning."

He poured a cup of coffee. "Good. That's what he needs to do."

I went upstairs and took a shower, all the while thinking about the words my mother said. Should I go to Boston? Both my parents seemed to think I should.

I wondered if Doc would mind if I flew the fancy plane there, or if I should make the four-hour trip by car.

"When are you leaving?" my father asked when I came back downstairs.

"Later. I'd like to see Jonas and his family before I go."

"Who knows when they might get here. Go ahead and leave. You can see them when you get back."

"Hey, Dad, you wanna tell me why you and Mom are so anxious to get me out of here?"

"It isn't that, son. We want you to be happy, and we both believe the key to that lies in a hospital bed in Boston, where she needs you as much as you need her."

"I've left messages. She hasn't picked up or returned my call."

"All the more reason to go. Find out why."

"I need to rent a car."

My dad tossed me a set of keys. "It's in the driveway."

I looked at the fob and saw the name of a well-known car rental company. I smiled and shook my head. "You have all the answers, don't you?"

He winked. "Always have, Gehring."

39

Alegria

I wondered what time my parents might show up today.

"The doctor is making rounds now," said the nurse who came in to take my blood pressure.

If I were still in the hospital in Stamford, Mantis would be here in time to hear what the doctor had to say. Given how insistent my parents had been that I be moved to this hospital, I was surprised it didn't seem to be a priority for them. Didn't everyone know doctors made rounds early in the morning?

I moved the blanket and sheet from my legs and willed my toes to wiggle. "Did you see that?" I asked the nurse.

"What?"

"I think my toes just moved."

The nurse stopped fiddling with the monitors. "Do it again," she said, watching my feet.

"Did you see it that time?"

"I sure did. The doctor will be so pleased with your progress."

I nodded, finding it ironic that my progress had nothing to do with this particular doctor, or with the hospital my parents had had me moved to. The feeling in my legs was coming back just like the doctor in Stamford had predicted.

"Good morning, Manon. How was your night?" The doctor was studying something on his computer and didn't seem to notice I hadn't responded to his question. "I see you believe you've had movement."

That was an interesting way to put it. "I wasn't alone in that belief."

"What's that? Oh, right," he said, again not waiting for a response. "Let's take a look."

He moved the blanket and sheet, and put pressure on different places on my legs and feet. I could feel all of it. There was less feeling in some areas than others, but for the most part, it was consistent.

I heard voices in the hallway and recognized my father's bellow. It sounded as though he was arguing with someone and was exasperated that they didn't know enough French to understand him. Both my parents spoke almost perfect English. I didn't know why they insisted on making whomever they were talking to, struggle to understand them.

My mother walked into the room, but didn't say anything. Much like the doctor, she didn't even look at me.

"Hello? Do you see a human being over here?"

"Stop being so dramatic, Manon," my mother snapped, opening a magazine and thumbing through the pages.

"I want to do another MRI this morning," the doctor told her.

"Is that healthy? I mean, radiation?"

"MRIs use magnetic frequency, not radiation," he muttered while making notes on the computer. "Someone from that department will come and get you soon."

Without asking if I had any questions, the doctor left the room. I caught the nurse shaking her head.

"I need to reschedule your physical therapy to later in the day," she said absentmindedly, sneaking looks over at my mother.

"*Maman*," I said. "Please return my phone to me."

"I don't know where it is," she said without looking up from the magazine.

"Yes, you do. Go back to the hotel and get it."

Her head snapped up. "*Pardon?*"

"I need my phone. Go get it."

My mother stared at me with her mouth open.

"Are you wondering about my manners, *Maman?* You shouldn't be. I've learned it wasn't necessary to use them from you and Papa."

"*Votre comportement,*" she mumbled, resting her gaze on the nurse as though she was suggesting their conversation shouldn't take place until the woman left the room.

I was accustomed to the nurses' routines and had a feeling the woman was stalling.

"Since you aren't needed here, I'm telling you to go back to your hotel, retrieve my phone, and return it to me."

My mother stood, but I doubted it was to do as I'd asked. She left the room, and soon I heard her telling my father about my behavior.

"You'd think I was a child," I muttered.

"Is there anything I can do?"

"I really need my phone," I answered just as the phone near my bedside rang.

"Hello?"

"Hey there. You aren't an easy person to get a hold of."

I was so relieved to hear Doc's voice. "I don't have my phone."

"I see. How are you feeling?"

"Better. I have movement in my legs. Not a lot, but enough that I'm encouraged." I didn't bother explaining that I hadn't before. There was no question Mantis had briefed Doc about my condition.

"I had a dream about Dutch. A nightmare."

"Yeah?"

"He was in trouble."

"Interesting."

"Have you been able to reach him?"

"I haven't, but I don't have any reason to believe—"

"I'm asking you to make sure he isn't in danger."

"I have every intention of continuing to do so."

"Thanks," I murmured, unsure if he was angry.

"Now I have a question for you."

"Go ahead."

"Is there a reason you didn't inform Mantis that you were changing hospitals?"

"It wasn't intentional. My parents..."

"I would be very disappointed to think you were refusing to communicate with him. We're a team, Alegria, and must operate as such regardless of any inappropriate relationships you may be in."

It felt as though Doc was scolding me, and I didn't like it. "As I said before, I don't have my phone," I snapped while glaring at my mother who had walked back into the room with my father.

"Alegria, is this a good time for you to talk more candidly?" Doc asked.

"It really isn't."

"Roger that. Please call me back when you're able to."

"Yes, sir, but I'll need your number," I answered. I felt my cheeks heat at having to ask for it, but until I was able to find my phone, I had no choice.

40

Dutch

I studied the man who stood before me, weighing his threat. "What do you want?"

When the man didn't answer, I sat down on the edge of the bed and rested my hand on the blanket that covered the naked woman's body. "Is this who you're here for? I can tell you, if she pleases you half as well as she pleased me, you'll be a happy man."

"*Silence!*" the man ordered. "You know who I want, and it isn't a whore."

"Enlighten me."

"Mantis Cassman. If he isn't here within twenty-four hours, you're a dead man."

Who the hell was Mantis Cassman?

I studied the man who had been guarding me for the last hour, and watched as he began to nod off. *That's what happens when you hire amateurs,* I thought to myself.

I almost had the rope binding my hands loose, and once it was, I'd be able to get to the knife I felt in the lining of my boot. Again, amateurs. They took my gun, but hadn't bothered to look for any other weapons.

Once I got my hands free and slit the throat of my so-called guard, I had to figure out how to get out of a hotel I had no memory of walking into.

41

Mantis

"You're sure she's at Spaulding?" I asked Doc.

"Talked to her a little over an hour ago."

That would've been the answer had I asked when Doc had spoken to Alegria, but it wasn't.

"She doesn't have her phone."

"What do you mean?"

"I had to call her hospital room."

"Outstanding." I smiled. "What is it?"

"Third floor, room ten. She had no idea you were trying to reach her, or so she said."

I'd spent the ten minutes before I called Doc, arguing with the woman at the information desk about whether they had a patient by the name of Manon Mondreau. She insisted they didn't. Now I knew they did.

I punched the button for the elevator and waited impatiently. Maybe I should've taken the stairs. As I was about to leave to do so, it dinged and I hopped on.

When the door reopened on the third floor, I stepped out and came face-to-face with Pierre Mondreau.

"Excuse me," I said when Alegria's father stepped in front of me.

"Manon does not wish to see you."

"You're under the assumption that I believe you." I maneuvered around him.

Pierre grabbed my arm. "I forbid it."

I laughed. "Take your hand off of me, or you'll experience the full force of how angry I am that you've kept her from getting in touch with me."

Her father scowled while still gripping my arm. "It's your fault she's paralyzed. Does that mean nothing to you? Have you so little regard for her safety?"

I hesitated for only a split second. "I don't answer to you." I shoved past him and stalked to the room number Doc had given me. When I stepped inside, I saw the bed was empty.

"Shit." Where the hell was she?

"Psst," I heard someone say, and saw a nurse motioning at me from across the hall.

When I stepped forward, she held up her hands to stop me from coming closer. "She's downstairs in radiology," she whispered. "Go that way." She pointed in the opposite direction from where I'd come. "First floor, turn right, and then left."

I mouthed my thanks, hurried down the hallway, and shoved open the door to the stairwell. If I'd come that way in the first place, I might've been able to avoid Manon's father entirely.

I'd just rounded the second corner and walked through the double doors that led to the radiology department when I saw her.

"Mantis?" Her eyes filled with tears.

"Hey there, Flygirl."

"You came."

I knelt down next to the wheelchair. "I would've been here sooner had I known you fled the state."

"I'm sorry…my parents…"

"Hey," I said, brushing her hair from her forehead. "I was kidding."

"I'm sorry I was so…horrible…to you."

I'd make another joke about how I was used to it, but right now, she wouldn't find it funny.

"You weren't horrible. You were in a car accident, Alegria."

"I hate it when I act like them."

"Who? Your parents?"

She nodded.

"Can I see your wristband, please?" asked a guy in scrubs who walked through the same double doors that I'd come through.

She lifted her arm.

"Manon? Is that how you pronounce it?"

She nodded.

"That's a beautiful name."

"Thanks," she murmured.

"A beautiful name for a beautiful woman," I whispered.

"Ready to get back to your room?" the orderly asked.

"Not really," she groaned.

"Why?" he asked.

Alegria looked up at me. "My parents might be up there."

"I saw them. Actually, I only saw your father."

"And?"

"I leveled him. He's probably in the emergency room as we speak."

She gasped. "You aren't serious?"

"No. I'm not. Although it was tempting."

"He's such a bastard," she spat.

The orderly appeared to be having a hard time holding in his laughter.

"Sorry," he said when he realized I'd noticed. "My dad is kind of a bastard too."

"Is he French?" Alegria asked.

"No. Why?"

"No one is more of a bastard than a Frenchman."

The orderly and I both laughed.

"What's your name?"

"Tom," he answered, pointing at his name badge that had been flipped, so I couldn't read it.

"Tom..." Alegria murmured and then rested her hand on my arm. "Have you heard from Dutch?"

I shook my head.

"Where do you want to go?" Tom asked.

"Do I have a choice?"

"Heck, yeah. You hungry? We can take a side trip to the cafeteria if you want."

"I'm starving, actually," she said, smiling.

Would her smile go away if I told her, right now, how much I loved her?

"*Oh, wait! Stop!*"

"*What?*"

"Look," she said, lifting the blanket covering her legs. She smiled up at me and wiggled her toes.

"Would you mind excusing us for a minute, Tom?"

"Sure thing, man. I'll be right around the corner."

I stood in front of her with my hands on the arms of the wheelchair. "There's something I want to do, but I don't want to upset you."

"What?" she whispered.

"I want to kiss you, Manon."

42

Alegria

It had been so long since I'd felt his lips on mine. There were times I thought I never would again. But before that could happen, there were so many things that needed to be resolved. First and foremost, was my relationship with Dutch. He may be avoiding me on purpose, but that didn't mean I could jump into a relationship with Mantis while I was still technically involved with him.

I reached out and touched Mantis' cheek with my fingertips. "I want that so much..." Should I tell him that, right before the car came crashing into the side of his dad's car, that I'd decided to end things with Dutch?

Mantis took his hands from either side of me and stood. "I'm sorry," he said, running his hand through his hair. "I keep crossing the line, even though I promised you I wouldn't."

"It isn't that I don't want to kiss you. It's—"

"Dutch. I get it."

"Please don't be angry with me. Not now. I can't bear it."

He knelt in front of me, cupped my cheek, and looked into my eyes. "Manon, you have to know that I love you. I never stopped loving you."

"I know," I whispered. "I still love you, too. Dutch knows that as well as we do. Maybe even better."

"Um...I just got paged for another pickup," said Tom from around the corner. "You two wanna go to the cafeteria now?"

"Can I take her?" Mantis asked.

"Only if you want me to lose my job."

"We don't want that. What do you say, Flygirl? Eat or face the firing squad?"

"Let's get it over with," I answered.

"Back to your room, then?" Tom asked.

I sighed. "Yes, please."

My stomach was in knots by the time the elevator opened on the third floor. Whatever relief I felt by not seeing my parents waiting in the hallway was soon replaced by dread that they were in my room.

When Tom wheeled me in, I saw my mother, but not my father.

"Manon," she said, nodding her head.

"*Maman.* You know Mantis, and this is Tom."

I almost giggled when Tom walked over to shake my mother's hand.

"Pleased to meet you, ma'am," he said. "You have a beautiful daughter."

My mother looked at me as if to confirm what Tom had said. Why did my own mother make me so uncomfortable?

"Thank you," I heard her say. "She is very beautiful."

"Thanks, *Maman*." I wondered briefly if this was just another crazy dream. Since when did my mother acknowledge something positive someone said about me?

"Bye now." Tom waved behind him, but then stuck his head back in the door. "I'll be back later to take you down to the cafeteria if you want."

I looked up at Mantis.

"I'll see if I can spring her myself, but thanks, Tom."

"Your father is arranging to have lunch brought in."

Now I was sure I was dreaming, and it pissed me off. I really wanted the words Mantis and I had said to each other to be real. I grabbed his hand and pulled him down.

"What's up?" he asked.

"I do love you, Mantis."

"And I love you. What's this about?" he whispered.

"I don't want this to be a dream."

He smiled and scrunched his eyebrows. "What makes you think you're dreaming?"

"Did you hear my mother say she thinks I'm beautiful and that my father is arranging for lunch?"

"Yeah." He grinned. "But did it occur to you how easy that would make it for him to poison me?"

43

Mantis

Alegria was mostly quiet until after her parents left, telling her they'd be back later.

"Thank God they're gone," she said once they walked out the door.

I had to admit they made me uncomfortable too, but at least they'd made some attempt to be civil. I certainly wouldn't have predicted their behavior after my confrontation with her father earlier.

"I had a dream about Dutch."

My eyes met hers. "Yeah?"

"He was in danger."

"Tell me about it."

She did, and the part that bothered me the most was that, in it, Dutch had said he was already dead. Sure, I'd had plenty of bizarre dreams that didn't mean a damn thing, but the words had sent a chill up my spine.

"I know Doc is working on making contact," she said. "But I'm worried."

I was too. Should I admit that to her or remind her that Dutch going dark was just part of the mission?

"Doc informed me that, as far as he knew, Dutch was in Germany. He has no reason to believe he is no longer there."

"Do you think he's refusing to make contact just because of us?"

"I don't." I shook my head. "Dutch may be pig-headed, or a know-it-all, but he isn't stupid. At the very minimum, he'd check in with Doc, even if he is 'bravely' letting you and I have space."

Alegria nodded, but still looked troubled.

"Talk to me, Flygirl."

"My instincts are telling me it's more than that."

"Let's call Doc together, then."

"You don't think I'm overreacting?"

"Never."

She reached over and put her hand on top of mine. "I appreciate that."

I wondered if I was about to make a mistake by telling her about my conversation with my mom, but I did it anyway. "My mom asked me to give her my top five words to describe you this morning."

"Are you going to tell me what you said?"

"Smart, stubborn, independent, and sexy as hell."

"That's only four."

"I know..."

"You have to tell me the fifth. If you weren't prepared to do so, you shouldn't have brought it up."

"Insecure."

Alegria looked away. "I am all those things."

"I'd always trust you to have my back, Flygirl. Always. I want you to know that. I trust your instincts as much as my own."

"And I, you. Let's call Doc."

By the time we hung up, Doc had reassured us that he'd stepped up the efforts to find Dutch, but would add a few more feet on the ground.

"We have operatives around the world on the lookout for him," he'd said.

The fact that no one had seen him was troubling in itself.

I held both of Alegria's hands in mine. "Look at me, Manon," I said. "I don't want to leave you…"

"But you have to."

"Not yet, but if Doc says the word, I'll have to go."

"I told Dutch before he left for Somalia that I understood he had to go in and get you. I also told him that if the situations were reversed, I'd understand and support your decision to do the same."

"And you understand I'm not choosing him over you."

"You are choosing me over him," she murmured. "You're choosing us."

I leaned forward and kissed her forehead. God, I missed the feel of her next to me so much. I'd do anything to feel her lips on mine, her arms around me, and being inside her, our bodies joined together.

She smiled. "I can read your thoughts."

"Good, then I don't have to say any of it out loud."

Alegria brought my hand to her lips. "I ache for you, Mantis."

"I love you, Manon."

"I love you, Gehring."

How long had it been since she'd called me by my first name? Since we were at pilot training, I'd guess. Even before that, she called me Cassman more than Gehring.

"I wish I could read your thoughts as easily as you can read mine," I said.

"I want everything you do. Maybe even more than you do." She pulled back and looked into my eyes. "When you left the hospital in Stamford, I wished we'd made love one more time, so I could remember."

"I can't tell you how many times I wished the same thing. There were times I wasn't sure I'd ever see you again, let alone make love to you."

"Mantis..."

"Talk to me. Whatever you have to say, I want to hear."

"Tell me what happened in Afghanistan."

I stood and walked toward the door.

"Where are you going?"

"Nowhere." I closed the door behind me and walked back over to her. "Are you sure you want to hear this?"

"I am."

"I haven't told anyone else..."

She nodded. "I understand."

* * *

It had been eight months, twelve days, and fifteen hours since I arrived in Kabul, and countless times I'd thought I was close to finding Bagish Safi.

I had no reason to believe my cover had been blown; I wouldn't have the access I had now if it had. I was rarely without the heavy makeup that convinced the terrorist organization I was Yousef Jamil, an Afghani native and Taliban supporter.

Once a day, I'd remove my disguise, shower, and then immediately reapply it. I had to be ready to act in a moment's notice and couldn't afford the risk not to be.

My initial access to al-Qaeda had been arranged by Islamic State leader Abdul Ghafor, a man to be feared far more than Bagish, but for now, the only person with plants—made up of former Taliban loyalists and now defectors—far enough inside his nemesis organization to get me in.

The closest I'd gotten to Bagish's inner circle was his nephew Abed Omar. Gaining Abed's trust had been a huge milestone in my mission to find and kill the man's uncle. Whether Abed was loyal to him or was one of Ghafor's secret followers, remained to be seen.

I hoped that soon everything I'd planned and worked for would finally happen, and then I'd be on my way back to the States while Bagish would be headed straight to hell.

The call came in at zero three hundred, alerting me that the Taliban was scheduled to gather with Afghan forces in the Rodat district of the eastern Afghan province of Nangarhar.

This meeting posed a significant threat to the Islamic State and was of enough importance that Bagish's attendance was expected.

Shortly after the group from Kabul arrived in Nangarhar, a suicide bomber almost derailed my mission. Thirty-six people were killed and another sixty-five had been injured in the bombing—Bagish among them. Instead of thwarting my mission, the bombing and ensuing chaos gave me the one shot I'd been waiting for, but I didn't use my gun to kill Bagish.

* * *

"I saw him lying there, barking orders at the one or two men still alive, and whose condition appeared much worse off than Bagish's. I was overcome by a rage unlike any I've ever felt. He thought I was coming to help him. Instead, I put a knife in his heart and watched him bleed out."

"Why was it so important that you kill Bagish?"

"He was the last direct link to Ian's death."

Alegria closed her eyes. "What happened next?"

"I didn't go back to Kabul. I connected with one of the men on Shiver's MI6 team, who arranged transport to the UK."

* * *

I had no idea how many days I'd been holed up in the London hotel room—maybe four or five? I'd chased off anyone, other than room service, who came to my door, and I'd refused access even to them.

"Leave it," I'd holler from my side of the door, and they would. Once word got out about the generosity of the tips I left, not a single bellman would question my demands.

When I heard the knock midmorning, I figured it was housekeeping and they hadn't seen, or chose to ignore, my do not disturb sign.

"Go away," I shouted, filling my glass with whiskey. I'd stopped bothering with ice after my first few hours, and while each bottle was delivered with a bucket of it, I let it melt.

"Mantis," said the familiar voice. "You can open the door and let me in, or I'll use the master key the manager so graciously gave to me."

"Go away, Shiver."

"Cannot do. Open the damn door."

* * *

"How did he convince you to come home?" Alegria asked.

I didn't remember anything other than it involved a lot more drinking, followed by Shiver sharing the outcome of a mission that had nearly destroyed his career.

His reason for revenge had been entirely different than mine, but that didn't change the fact that an op undertaken with a reason other than the mission was destined to either fail or destroy the operative.

In both cases, the mission hadn't failed, but had taken a great toll on the man who carried it out.

44

Alegria

I watched Mantis' face as he told me the story he'd never told anyone else. His pain sat so close to the surface, I could feel it.

All those years, it had been about avenging his brother's death. Why hadn't he ever said so? The better question was, why hadn't I sensed it?

"That's what it was. The reason you accepted every mission put in front of you."

Mantis nodded.

"How many others?"

He shrugged. No one liked to keep track of the number of people they'd killed, myself included.

"Too many, including a couple locked up in Guantanamo." He shook his head. "I was lost," he whispered. "I still am."

I pulled him close. "Lie with me." When he was by my side in the small hospital bed, I wrapped my arms around him.

"You aren't lost anymore, Mantis."

I brought my lips to his and softly kissed him.

"Manon." He groaned.

"Shh. Don't talk. We've both talked enough."

Mantis pulled me closer, so my head rested on his chest.

45

Dutch

The naked woman from the hotel room must've lifted my wallet, either that or the terrorists had. That's the way I'd started thinking of them.

Whoever they were, they wanted me to deliver someone called Mantis. Since I had no idea who that was, I'd have a damn hard time doing it.

I looked around once I was out on the street. I was in Germany, that much was obvious, but who I was and why I was here, wasn't.

No identification. No money. No idea if there was anyone I could turn to for help. I was as far up shit creek as I could get.

My only hope was that there was someone looking for me—people on my side. I already knew the bad guys were, but how would I know the difference?

The only things I had now were my instincts and my life. In order to keep the latter, I had to rely on the former.

I caught someone watching me out of the corner of my eye and ducked into the nearest alley. From there I saw the man pull out a phone, talk for a couple of minutes, and then walk in my direction.

If he was a bad guy, wouldn't he have come directly after me rather than make a phone call first?

I pulled out my knife, prepared for my instincts to be wrong, and waited until the man came around the corner, but he never did.

46

Mantis

When I woke, I was still in the small hospital bed, next to Alegria. My muscles ached, but my heart felt better than it had in months.

Holding her in my arms felt like coming home, but hearing Alegria say she loved me was like being reborn. The life I was afraid I'd never have was within reach. All I had to do was be patient, find Dutch, and tell him that he'd been right all along.

This time around, I'd do things differently. Before I accepted any mission, including one involving Dutch, I'd discuss it with her. I didn't want to give Alegria any reason to doubt that she mattered more to me than anyone or anything—including avenging my brother's death.

The need to wasn't gone entirely; it had just changed. Like I'd told her, I felt lost, as though I wasn't sure what the purpose of my life was anymore.

With Alegria by my side, we'd forge a new life together instead of alone.

She shifted, murmuring in her sleep. "Mantis?"

"Yes, sweetheart?"

"Am I dreaming?"

"You're not."

"Good." She snuggled in closer. "I want to walk today."

I didn't know if her legs were strong enough for her to be able to, but I'd do everything I could to help her. "Sounds great."

"I want to get out of the hospital too."

"Let's hear what the doctor says this morning and see if we can make both happen."

"If Doc believes Dutch is in danger, I want to go in with you."

I could've predicted Alegria would say those exact words. If I were the one whose medical clearance was questionable, I'd do everything I could to get healthy. The idea of a team going in without me, particularly for one of our own, would never sit right with me.

"I understand."

"But..."

"No buts. It's up to you, sweetheart. I'm your... um... I'm not your dad." I'd come so close to saying I was her boyfriend, but I wasn't yet—not until we were able to reach Dutch.

She nodded against my chest, her hair tickling my neck.

"The thing that worries me most is that whatever trouble he's in, is because of me," I admitted.

"It could be because of any of us. We've all had ops that required us to do things we knew would result in our heads being on the block."

I nodded. She was right, but something was telling me that I was more right.

"Dr. Gertman is in surgery this morning. I'm Dr. Perry."

I shook the man's extended hand, as did Alegria.

"I understand the feeling in your legs is slowly returning." He moved the sheet that covered her. "Nod when you feel my fingers."

Everywhere the doctor rested his hands, Alegria nodded. When he told her to try moving, she was able to.

"I'd like to walk today."

The doctor murmured his agreement. "I see no reason why you shouldn't be able to."

"What about the neuropathy?" I asked. "She was having issues before her last surgery."

The doctor studied her chart. "I see there were fragments removed. Are these bullet fragments?" he asked, raising his eyebrows.

"Yes," answered Alegria.

He ran a pen on the bottom of her left foot. She flinched and giggled.

"We'll try some more uh...scientific tests this afternoon, but I'm optimistic."

"I'd like to be discharged."

The doctor looked first at Alegria and then at me. "If we allow this, what kind of help will you have?"

I wanted to tell the doctor that I'd be by her side no matter what, but I couldn't. If Doc called and said I was needed, I would have to leave.

"My parents are here," she answered. "They'll hire someone if need be."

My gaze met hers and she smiled. Alegria was telling me that if I had to go, she'd make arrangements for me to be able to.

"I'll need to consult with Dr. Gertman, but let's see if we can get you out of here today."

"I love your smile," I told her after the doctor had left.

Her cheeks turned pink. "It feels like it's been a while since I've felt like smiling."

47

Alegria

"Mantis is making arrangements for a place to stay, but he'll be back later. In the meantime, there are a few things I want to talk to you about," I told my parents when they arrived an hour after Mantis had left.

I'd been sitting in a wheelchair by the window when they arrived, and instead of moving closer to them, I stayed where I was.

"I'm listening," said my father.

"First of all, I need a way to communicate, so unless you know where my phone is and can return it to me, I need you to get me another."

"Matille," said my father, turning to my mother, who reached into her bag and set my cell on the tray table.

I rolled the wheelchair closer and picked it up.

"Thank you. Next, I need the best damn physical therapists money can buy. If they aren't here, I want you to arrange for me to be moved to wherever they are."

I watched as my father again met my mother's gaze.

"If you can't help me—"

My father held up his hand. "We will."

"Good." I shook my head. "Thank you."

My father nodded and looked at my mother yet again.

"Why do you keep checking with her?" I snapped.

"And you," I said to my mother, "are you going to deny my father helping me?"

"Manon." He stood and rested his hand on my shoulder. "There's something your mother and I need to tell you."

I moved the wheelchair away so I was out of his reach. "What?"

"Your condition is not the only reason we're in Boston."

I heard my mother's voice catch, and when I looked, I saw her brush away tears.

"What's going on?"

"Your mother is here for treatment as well."

"What for?"

"I have recently been diagnosed with pancreatic cancer," she answered, barely above a whisper.

I looked between them. "When did you find out?"

"A few weeks ago, but it wasn't until yesterday that we found out how advanced the disease is."

I hated that the first thing I'd thought upon hearing the news was that it explained why my parents had suddenly been so much nicer to me.

I wheeled over and took my mother's hand. *"Je suis désolée, Maman."* I looked at my father. "This changes everything."

"What do you mean?" my mother asked.

"You and Papa need to focus on your health. I will manage on my own."

My mother shook her head. *"Non."*

"Manon," my father began, pulling a chair over to sit near my mother. "It is important to your *maman* that we do whatever we can to help you heal."

"What about you?"

"It may be too late for me," my mother answered, squeezing my fingers.

"You can fight this. You can beat it."

"Manon." My father shook his head.

"You can't just give up," I insisted, looking into my mother's eyes.

"I'm not giving up." She sighed and then looked at my father. "Pierre, may I talk with our daughter alone, *s'il vous plaît?*"

He nodded and walked out of the room.

"The disease is advanced, Manon. The doctors said they would do everything they could to keep me comfortable." She took a deep breath. "I'm sorry."

I shook my head and wiped away my tears.

"My biggest regret is that I have not been a better mother to you. I know it's too late..."

"No. It isn't," I cried. "The cancer...there are treatments..."

"Not the cancer, *ma fille*. I know I can never make the time we missed up to you."

"There is nothing to make up, *Maman*."

She smiled and nodded. "There is too much, but for whatever time I have left, I want to try."

"You can't worry about me. You have to focus on yourself."

"I have spent all of my life, and most of yours, focused on myself. Now I want to focus on you."

I heard a knock on the door. "Can you give us a few more minutes?" I asked the nurse walking in.

"I need to get you hooked back up to the monitors. It'll only take a minute."

"It's okay," said my mother. "Do as she asks."

I wheeled over to the bed, and the nurse lowered it.

"Can you manage, or should I call for someone to help?"

"I can manage." I could move my legs, but that didn't mean I had enough strength to use them to support myself. Instead, I used my arms to shift from the wheelchair to the bed.

Once I settled, the nurse began reattaching the leads from the monitors to my body.

"Where did my mother go?" I asked when the nurse moved out and I saw the chair where she'd been sitting was empty.

"I don't know," the nurse answered. "She was just here a second ago."

I closed my eyes, rested my head against the pillow, and pulled my phone out of the pocket of my hospital gown. I expected it to be dead, but instead, it was fully charged. I punched in my passcode and saw that my screen background had been changed. Instead of a photo of an F15 in flight, there was one of me with my mother when I was a baby. I had no idea how my parents had figured out the code to get into my cell, but it didn't matter. I held it close to my heart, wishing my mother would come back so I could hold her close instead.

48

Mantis

I'd been back less than an hour when my phone buzzed. "It's Doc," I told Alegria and put it on speaker.

"I got word from Shiver," Doc began. "Rivet swears he saw Dutch in Kaiserslautern."

"Did he make contact?" Alegria asked.

"Negative."

"Why not?" I asked.

"He said that Dutch looked right at him and then ducked into an alley," answered Doc.

"So he assumed Dutch didn't want him to approach."

"Something like that. Rivet mentioned it in passing during a phone call with Shiver."

Rivet was Shiver's boss at MI6—wouldn't he have been privy to the bulletins about Dutch?

"What's Rivet doing in Kaiserslautern?" I asked.

"On holiday."

At least that explained why Rivet hadn't known about Dutch being MIA.

"Listen, Mantis, there's chatter about Zamed Safi. Word is he's on the hunt."

I nodded, my gaze focusing on Alegria's. "For me," I murmured.

"Affirmative," Doc answered.

No one had considered Zamed, Bagish and Dadvar Safi's youngest brother, a threat. His dossier read "student of philosophy" and didn't list a tie to the Taliban, the Islamic State, or al-Qaeda, other than his two brothers.

"Who's backing him?" I asked.

"Unknown."

"What's his purported threat level?" asked Alegria.

"Again, unknown. I'll be back in touch when I know more about Dutch and about Safi. For now, sit tight."

"Tell me what you're thinking," I said to Alegria after disconnecting the call.

"It might be a good idea to contact Razor," she suggested.

Everyone who'd ever worked with him knew Razor Sharp, third founding partner of K19, never forgot a face. Nor did he forget any details he'd ever learned about a person.

"I heard Zamed was Bagish's personal secretary, translator, and press spokesman," Razor told us. "In addition to his native Pashto, he speaks English, Arabic,

Urdu, and Persian. He was born in Jelahor village, Arghandab District, Kandahar Province."

"What threat level would you consider him?"

"I'd say minimal. Without the power of his two older brothers behind him—you know, since they're dead—he doesn't carry much weight. The vendetta, if it's true he has one, would be personal. He wouldn't be acting on behalf of the Taliban."

"Enemies?" Alegria asked.

Razor laughed. "Everyone who rose to a position of power after Bagish's death."

"Because they see him as a threat?"

"Because they see everyone as a threat. Your best bet in terms of neutralizing the little bastard is to make Abdul Ghafor think he's after him too."

Given the leader of the Islamic State was integral in me infiltrating the Taliban back when I was after Bagish Safi, it wouldn't be a stretch for a rumor such as the one Razor was suggesting to be taken seriously. Going after *anyone*—K19, CIA, ISIL, or al-Qaeda—without the full force of the Taliban, was tantamount to a death wish.

It would be foolish, however, not to think Zamed had the means to assassinate me. Anyone with access to a deadly weapon could make it happen.

"Someone should just take him out. Make sure the evil bloodline ends with this generation of Safis," Razor said before ending the call. "By the way, is Doc putting a team together?"

"Not yet."

"When he does, I want to handle it."

"Roger that," I answered, unsure why Razor wanted to do so, but I wouldn't argue.

"I guess now I wait," I said after we ended the call.

Alegria nodded. "I can't wait to find out whether I'm getting out of this place."

I smiled and stroked her cheek with my finger. "I get that you're Superwoman—you always have been—but I'm not sure it's wise to spring you while you're still hooked up to all this." I motioned to the various monitors keeping track of her vital signs along with the IV she was still attached to.

"Spoilsport."

Alegria looked away, but I could see the tears in her eyes.

I put my fingers on her chin and turned her head so she'd look at me. "Tell me why you're crying."

She shook her head.

"If you won't tell me, I can't help make it better."

"I'm not sure anyone can make it better."

I wiped her tears with my finger, but they didn't stop falling.

"It's my mom."

"What about her?"

Alegria reiterated her conversation with her parents.

"I'm so sorry, sweetheart." I lay next to her on the bed and put my arms around her.

"Once the nurse came in, my mom just left. I haven't heard from her since."

"How long ago was this?"

"About an hour before you got back."

"Do you want me to try to reach your dad?"

"Would you mind?"

"Of course not."

Alegria handed me her phone. When her father didn't answer the call, I left a message.

"Knock, knock. Are you two lovebirds at it again?" we heard Tom say from the doorway.

I stood. "Come on in."

"I'm here to take the beautiful lady to physical therapy. You comin' along?"

"Sure am."

"Glad to hear it. Patients always do better when they have family there to help."

"I'll be here every day as long as she'll let me."

Alegria smiled, but we both knew it wasn't entirely up to her. When the call came from Doc, saying I was needed, I'd have to leave.

I could tell how hard Alegria was trying to fool the physical therapist into thinking her legs were stronger than they were.

"I just want to get out of the damn hospital and get on with my life," she said. "Why can't my body cooperate?"

"If you push too hard, you'll only wind up in worse shape than you are now."

When Alegria stuck her tongue out as he walked away, I was smart enough to keep my mouth shut, although I was tempted to remind her she hadn't been any different with me all those years ago when I was recovering from surgery.

"We're done for today," said the same therapist who had warned her about working too hard.

Without him saying so, I knew he wouldn't recommend that she go home this afternoon, especially after he told her he'd see her the next day.

"I'm sorry, sweetheart," I said after the therapist told her it was okay to return to her room.

"You might not want to stick around tonight," she muttered.

"Why's that?"

"I'm warning you in advance that I'm going to be lousy company."

I smiled, stopped the chair, walked around in front of her, and kissed her forehead.

"What's that for?" she asked.

"Because sometimes you need love the most when you think you deserve it the least."

"What does that mean?"

"It means you're never as unlovable as you think."

"I don't think I'm unlovable," she said when the elevator dinged and I pushed her inside.

"You're also not lousy company."

"You might change your mind."

I laughed. "After spending so much time without you in my life, there isn't much you can do to make me want to leave."

"Not much, huh?"

I stood when we heard a knock on the door, and walked over to open it.

"Okay, lovebirds," said Tom. "Time for dinner."

One of the nurses followed Tom in and disconnected the leads to the monitors as well as hung the IV from the pole on the wheelchair.

"Where are we going?" Alegria asked.

"You'll see."

She gasped when Tom wheeled her through a door near the cafeteria entrance. "What's all this?"

The private dining room was set up with a single table for two. The rest of the surrounding tables were laden with candles and vases filled with roses.

"Would you like to take it from here?" Tom asked.

"Sure would." I wheeled her to the table, and a man came through a different door, carrying two plates that he set in front of each of us.

"I'd like to tell you that we prepared this in the hospital kitchen, but sadly, we did not," the man said before going back through the same door.

"Wow." Alegria gasped, looking over the assortment of cheese, fruit, and artisan breads. "Do you think my father arranged for this?"

I smiled. "Do you?"

She shrugged. "It seems a bit overkill."

Three more courses were served before she solved the mystery.

Alegria smiled when the man set individual Pavlovas in front of us. "This was not arranged by my father."

I rested my chin in my palm. "No?"

"You did this."

"What makes you think so?"

"The details."

"Go on."

"Don't play coy. You know very well that raspberries, kiwi, and blueberries are my three favorite fruits. You also know I am a stickler for a perfectly toasted, crispy meringue."

"A stickler, huh?"

"Shut up," she said, smiling.

"I know it was difficult to find out you couldn't leave the hospital tonight."

She reached across the table for my hand. "Thank you."

I stood, moved my chair closer to the wheelchair, and took her hands in mine. "I love you, and I want to spend my life with you. I hope you know that. No matter what happens."

"I want that too, Mantis."

"You and Dutch…"

"We're more friends than lovers."

I closed my eyes. "I don't know that I'll ever be able to talk about the lover part—or listen to you talk about it."

"We don't have to talk about it. I just want you to know that my relationship with him wasn't...the same."

"As what?"

She looked into my eyes. "I could never love another man the way I love you."

My phone vibrated, but I ignored it. "I feel the same way about you."

"See who it is," she said when the phone continued to vibrate.

"It's Doc." I brought the cell to my ear.

"I hope I'm not interrupting anything."

"Alegria and I are just finishing a romantic dinner."

"Shit," he muttered. "That makes it harder for me to tell you why I'm calling."

"Go ahead."

"Onyx, Monk, and Striker are on their way to Boston. They'll meet you at the airfield, and you'll fly out together. Diesel and Ranger are already on their way. Gunner, Razor, and I are on standby."

"Things have escalated."

"Striker will brief you when you arrive."

"Roger that."

"Almost a full team," Alegria said when I ended the call with Doc, obviously having overheard the details of the conversation.

I nodded. "I can't believe I'm leaving you already."

49

Dutch

I scrubbed my face with my hand. I was getting damn hungry, not to mention it would soon be nightfall and I had nowhere to stay. Maybe my best bet would be to check into a hospital and tell them I'd lost my memory. Either that or go to a police station.

Only the idea that whoever had me held captive earlier would be looking in those two places first kept me from doing it.

"Dutch?" I heard someone say.

I probably wouldn't have even noticed, but the woman's voice sounded so familiar. I turned around, hoping she wasn't about to put a gun in my side, and was met by the prettiest hazel eyes I'd ever seen.

"I've been looking for you," she whispered. "Everyone is."

I pulled her around a corner into another alley. "Who are you?" I asked.

"Come with me." She pulled me farther into the alley. The grip I had on her arm obviously didn't bother her.

She used a key card to open an unmarked door and dragged me inside with her. She put a finger over her lips and motioned me toward an elevator.

I sure as hell hoped she was one of the good guys, but if I had to die, at least the last face I'd see was a damn pretty one.

When the elevator reopened, she grabbed my hand and led me down the hallway, using the same key card to open another door.

"Who are you?" I asked again once we were inside.

"Would you be able to answer the same question?"

I smiled. "I don't know who the hell you are, but you sure are beautiful."

She laughed. "And there we have the answer."

"What?"

"You don't know who you are."

"No, sweetheart," I said, shaking my head. "But instead of finding out, I'd rather get to know you better."

"Your personality is still intact."

"What did you call me earlier? Dutch?"

She nodded and walked to a table that was just inside the entryway.

I looked around. "Nice place."

"Thanks. It's not mine."

"Whose is it?"

"Company apartment. Take a seat."

"Hmm, bossy. I like it."

She shook her head, but was still smiling. "What's the last thing you remember?"

"Before I answer that, tell me who you are."

She reached down under her pant leg, pulled something out, and handed it to me.

"Special Agent Malin Kilbourne," I read on the CIA badge. I tossed it on the table, stood, and walked over to the refrigerator. "You got anything to eat in here, special agent?"

"Fresh out of spaghetti and meatballs, I'm afraid."

"Ah. So you know what I like to eat." I turned around and looked into her eyes. "Please tell me we aren't related."

She laughed and joined me next to the refrigerator. "No, Dutch, we aren't related."

"But we have a past."

"We do."

"A complicated one."

"Your instincts are amazingly sharp."

"Right," I said, sitting back down. "Tell me what you know."

"You've been in Germany approximately seven days. Doc has been trying to reach you for the last six...Does that name mean anything to you?"

I shook my head as I watched her pull food out of the refrigerator. I wasn't sure which I wanted more—to know who I was, something to eat, or to get Malin Kilbourne naked.

Her hair was pulled back, but it looked long and inky black. Her hazel eyes and curvaceous body were as equally stunning as her pretty face. My guess was that when she was naked, her hair spread out on the pillow beneath her head, and her eyes hooded in pleasure—she was breathtaking.

"You're feeding me, so I guess you like me."

"That might be a stretch."

"Complicated bad, then."

She smiled and nodded.

"Tell me this much, was the sex good?"

"Off the charts."

"That's what I like to hear." I rubbed the back of my head where I'd been hit. "You wanna check this out for me, Special Agent Kilbourne?"

"It doesn't look like you lost any blood along with your memory," she said after running her fingers over the bump.

"I like the feel of your fingers in my hair, Kilbourne."

"Don't push it, Dutch. I'm cutting you some slack because you're suffering from amnesia, but don't forget the part about our relationship being complicated bad."

"Roger that, so who's after me?"

"Our best guess is Zamed Safi."

"Name doesn't mean anything to me."

"Are there any names that mean something to you?"

I thought about it for a minute. "Nope."

"Where have you been for the last week?"

"It's fuzzy, but I woke up in a hotel room, with... uh...a naked woman next to me—"

"Doesn't sound out of the ordinary so far."

"As I was saying, shortly after I woke up, some gun-toting guy and his armed posse stormed into the room."

"What happened next?"

I was about to make a joke about offering him the naked woman, but something told me she wouldn't appreciate my humor. "He wanted me to deliver someone called Mantis."

"I see."

"What do you see?"

"Your story pretty much confirms that it was Safi. How'd you end up wandering the streets?"

"Safi ain't exactly a pro, if you know what I'm sayin'. The one guard he left on my watch fell asleep, and no one even checked to see what weapons I had on me."

"How were you able to free yourself."

I pulled a knife out of my boot.

"And the guard?"

"I guess I should've slit his throat."

"But you didn't?"

"Negative."

She put a bowl of soup on the table along with bread and butter.

"Is this for me?"

She nodded and looked at something on her phone. "I need to check in and give an update on your whereabouts and condition."

"I'm pretty beat. Is there a place where I can crash for a bit after I eat?"

Kilbourne pointed to a sofa on her way out of the room.

"Thanks," I muttered.

Someone crashing through the door of the apartment woke me up from where I slept on the sofa. I reached for the weapon I already guessed wasn't there, right before someone hit me over the head—again.

I was in and out of consciousness as they dragged me through the battered door; I heard someone speaking in Arabic say there wasn't anyone else in the apartment.

"Fuck," I muttered as blackness engulfed me again. Had pretty little Special Agent Kilbourne betrayed me?

50

Mantis

Striker was in what appeared to be an intense conversation with Onyx when I arrived at the airfield. I hung back until Striker motioned me over.

"How's Alegria?" he asked.

"Doing better. She's getting feeling back in her legs."

"She didn't have feeling in her legs?" Onyx asked.

"She did, but she was experiencing some neuropathy," I said when both men looked as though they expected me to elaborate.

"Wasn't there another accident?" Striker asked.

"Yeah. Snowstorm," I said as though that was the end of the explanation. "Is this our transport?" I pointed to one of K19's larger planes.

"Can you fly?" Onyx asked when I followed him on board.

"Yeah. I'm good."

"I'll take the first leg," he offered. "We'll go from here to JFK and then on to Kabul."

"Kabul? I thought Dutch was in Germany?"

"About that," said Striker, sitting down in the jump seat. "We got a report that he was seen with one of the agency's operatives. When they couldn't reach her, they sent someone in. Found her place ransacked, no sign of her or Dutch."

"Who?"

"Malin Kilbourne. You know her?"

I nodded.

"Don't make me ask," warned Striker.

"She and Dutch were...uh...connected for a while."

"What happened?"

"I disappeared."

"Yeah? What's that got to do with it?"

Was Striker serious right now? "Alegria, asshole."

"Got it. Sorry."

I watched as Striker thought through the missing agent's connection to Dutch. I could almost predict his next question.

"How mad was Kilbourne?"

"I can't tell you. She and Dutch were together when I left, and then when I got back, he was with Alegria."

"Roger that," Striker mumbled. "Like I said, she's missing too."

"Hey, Monk," I said when the last man we were waiting on boarded the plane. Monk nodded his head as he walked by.

I'd never known anyone who had a more appropriate code name than Rhys "Monk" Perrin. The man only spoke when absolutely necessary, and evidently saying hello wasn't.

"Let's get the briefing out of the way before we get in the air," Striker suggested.

I followed him into the main cabin and listened as Striker gave us a vector of the situation and laid out our operating plan.

"This isn't just about Dutch anymore, gentlemen. If we can't get in there and neutralize Zamed Safi, then a full-blown war is going to break out between the Islamic State and the Taliban."

"I thought Zamed was operating on his own."

"He is, but you know Ghafor. He's a paranoid schizophrenic."

I wasn't sure Abdul Ghafor was diagnosable as such, but I understood what Striker was saying. It wouldn't matter if Allah himself told him Zamed was acting outside of the Taliban; Ghafor probably wouldn't believe it.

"Zamed wants me," I said, looking each of the men in the eye. "I'm the target."

"I won't argue with you," Striker responded, "but as I said, it's bigger than you and Dutch. Zamed could start a chain reaction that would wind up as the worst war the Middle East has ever seen. The agency wouldn't consider direct involvement if that weren't the case."

Striker had retired from the CIA a few months prior and signed on as a K19 partner at the same level I would be when I finally got around to meeting with Doc. Striker, though, still had the closest ties to the agency, seconded by Doc. When I heard we were on our way to Kabul and that this was a CIA op, I knew that meant the agency was footing the bill. Our operating plan wouldn't differ much if it were an agency op or a K19 op, though.

"Let's go," Striker said, closing his laptop. "The sooner we're airborne, the sooner we can get the job done and get our asses back home."

I didn't know a lot about Striker other than that he was former CIA. I'd heard two rumors. First, that his family was screwed up to the point where, early on, their dubious associations had almost cost Striker his career. Secondly, he was involved with Aine McNamara, twin sister of Razor Sharp's wife, Ava. That wasn't as much of a rumor since I'd seen them together on Thanksgiving.

Based on Striker's impatience to get the op over with, I guessed that the relationship was still on.

"We'll talk more when we land at JFK."

"Roger that," I answered Striker.

The flight from Boston to JFK would be quick. However, JFK to Dubai would take over twelve hours, and then from Dubai to Kabul would take another three.

With everything going on with Alegria, my sleep hadn't been worth shit, and now, it would be at least fourteen hours, maybe even twenty, before I'd be able to bunk down.

Knowing Dutch was being held captive when it was really me that Zamed wanted, meant that even if I could close my eyes, I wouldn't sleep.

51

Alegria

Saying goodbye to Mantis was the hardest thing I'd ever done. Harder than any time before this. This time, if he got into trouble, I would be powerless to do anything to help him or the rest of the K19 team.

"You all right, miss?" Tom asked as he wheeled me back to my room after Mantis left.

I squared my shoulders. "I will be."

He gave me a fist pump. "That's what I like to hear. You tell me if there's anything I can do to help."

I opened my eyes; I must've drifted off. I raised my head and looked around my empty hospital room, already missing Mantis so much it hurt.

The other hurt that had settled square in my chest was my mother's news. No matter what she'd said the day before, my parents had to focus on her recovery, not on mine. Whatever energy my mother put forth on my behalf would only take away from her own battle.

Why did it always take some kind of illness or tragedy to bring people together?

Mantis and I found our way back to each other because I got shot and needed surgery. If I hadn't, who knew how long we might've gone before realizing what Dutch had been trying to tell us all along? Would I have remained stubbornly waiting for some grand gesture on Mantis' part, or would I have settled into a relationship with Dutch, one in which we both would've ended up miserable?

"Good morning," said the nurse I recognized from the night before.

"You're still here?"

"Only for about another hour." The woman checked the monitor leads to make sure they were still properly attached, straightened my bedding, and then rested her hand on my knee. "Feel that?"

I nodded.

"Good," she said, tucking the sheet and blanket under my legs. "Dr. Gertman will be in soon. Maybe another half an hour."

Like before, I wondered if either of my parents planned to be here when he made rounds; however, knowing what my mother was going through, I doubted they would.

Tom knocked on the door and came in with a vase of roses. "Special delivery," he said, setting the bouquet on the ledge by the window and then handing me the card.

Mon coeur,

Know that until I am with you again, able to touch your lips with mine, I will be thinking of you every minute of every day.

All my love, forever and ever,
Mantis

"By the look on your face, he must've written something pretty romantic."

I smiled.

"What brings you to the third floor this morning?" I asked. "Just flower delivery?"

"I need to ask where you want the rest of the flowers."

"What do you mean?"

"From last night. I have them on a cart outside the door."

"Oh. I don't know. I mean you can't bring them all in here."

"If you don't want them, I have another idea."

"By all means, please tell me."

"In a hospital like this one, there are a lot of people who stay more than a few days at a time. Some don't get many visitors, and after the first few days, they don't get flowers either."

"I like this idea."

"I'll set about delivering them if you agree."

"I do, and thank you, Tom."

"My pleasure, Miss Mondreau," he said, bowing a little.

"Please, call me Alegria."

"I thought your name was Manon," he said, looking at my wristband.

"It is, but my friends call me Alegria."

I could've sworn Tom blushed. "I'll be back to get you a little later, Miss Alegria," he said. "You have a rigorous rehab session scheduled this afternoon."

"Good. I'm ready."

52

Mantis

I landed the plane at Bagram Air Base, the largest US military installation in Afghanistan. It had been occupied by Afghan Armed Forces and the US-led Resolute Support Mission since 2002. In the time between, the base had grown to the size of a small town, housing over ten thousand troops and three thousand insurgent inmates in the detention facility.

Tonight we'd be staying at the base's Camp Vance, which had been established by the United States Department of Defense to headquarter the Combined Joint Special Operations Task Force.

The camp had been named for Gene Arden Vance Jr., a member of the US Special Forces and a cryptologic linguist who, despite being critically wounded, helped save the lives of two fellow Americans and eighteen Afghani soldiers during the hunt for Osama Bin Laden.

Along with Airborne Special Forces, the camp also provided headquarters for Army Special Forces, Infantry, a Marine Special Operations battalion, and a Navy SEAL team.

"Who all will be in on tomorrow's meeting?" I asked Striker.

"Wouldn't surprise me if God or the president showed up, given the number of other high-ranking officials you'll brief."

"What does that mean?"

"You heard right. There's a congressional panel arriving tonight, who along with most of the military brass, want to know every detail regarding the assassination of Bagish Safi."

"How much trouble am I in?"

"Trouble? Fuck, Mantis, you're a goddamn hero."

I didn't want to be a hero; heroes couldn't fly under the radar like I needed to. A hero wouldn't be able to walk out and offer himself up in exchange for Dutch like I'd planned to—not unless I could make it happen tonight, before tomorrow's briefing.

"We're gathering in the situation room at zero seven hundred," said Striker, handing me a room key card.

"Roger that."

"Get some rest, Mantis."

I nodded, but that's the last thing I planned to do. Thankfully, God must've heard my silent plea because when I rounded the corner, the one man who could help me carry out my plan, Abdul Ghafor, leader of the

Islamic State, stood directly in front of me. "Abdul," I said, "is this a coincidence, or have you been waiting for me?"

"I think you know the answer."

"We need to talk."

Ghafor nodded.

In less than an hour, I was being escorted out of Camp Vance in the back of Abdul's SUV, disguised as Bakr Al-Abudadi, Ghafor's number two.

53

Alegria

"I don't understand," I said when Doc called to tell me that Mantis had disappeared from Bagram Air Base.

"We believe he went over there with a plan. Did he say anything to you? Anything at all?"

He hadn't, but it wouldn't be hard to figure out what he intended to do. Even Doc had to have already guessed.

"He's offering himself up in exchange for Dutch's release."

Not surprisingly, Doc confirmed those were his same suspicions. "Who would he know that could help him make that happen?"

"It's a long shot, but what about Ghafor?"

"We've made contact. He sent word that he knows nothing about his whereabouts."

"He's lying."

"We're going in."

"Who is?"

"Razor, Gunner, and me."

I sat on the side of the bed, resting my feet flat on the floor. Yesterday, I'd been able to walk across the room twice. Tonight I'd have to go twice that far—once I convinced my parents to help me leave the hospital.

"Papa, I need your help. *Maman*, too," I said when he answered his phone.

"We were just on our way to the hospital."

"I see. Can you come here afterward?"

"I meant we were on our way to see you."

"Perfect," I said and hung up.

"I need to mobilize," I told my father when they arrived. "It's something I have to do, and while you may not understand why, I'm asking for your help anyway."

I looked over at my mother. "You said that you wanted to focus on our relationship. What I'm asking both of you is to support me in this, unconditionally."

"What is it you're proposing?" my father asked.

"First, I have to leave the hospital. This morning, Dr. Gertman told me it would be at least two or three more days before he'd be willing to release me. I need to leave tonight."

My father nodded.

"Next, I need to get to Afghanistan."

"Taller order," he answered, rubbing his chin. "I'll need to make arrangements for the aircraft."

"I meant to fly commercial, Papa."

He scowled and shook his head.

"I don't have flight clearance."

When he waved his hand in dismissal, I looked at my mother, who merely nodded.

"What else?" he asked.

"I haven't figured that out yet."

"What is your intention?"

"To get Mantis and Dutch out of Afghanistan."

"She is certainly your daughter, Pierre."

My father murmured something and nodded. "It'll take money."

I'd thought about that angle, but even if I used every penny I had and mortgaged my Manhattan apartment, it wouldn't be enough. "It'll take too much money."

"Give me twenty-four hours."

I raised my eyebrows when my father walked out of the room. "What just happened?"

"He's taking care of it."

"Just like that?"

"That's what your father does."

"I'm talking a lot of money, *Maman*."

"He understood what you meant, and it isn't a problem. Your father is very, very wealthy."

Did most adult children know their parents' net worth? "Why do you say he's very wealthy? Aren't you?"

She smiled. "I suppose I am, Manon. However, I am also French."

"Meaning?"

"Saying so would be...crass."

"Brace yourself, *Maman*, I'm going to be crass. When you say very, very...what are we talking?"

My mother sighed. "Your father is a billionaire, *ma fille*."

"Sorry, am I being too American for you?"

"Oui."

When my parents came back the next morning, my mother brought a change of clothes, and my father brought a plan of action.

While I changed into the clothes my mother had been wearing, my father explained that we would walk to the elevator together while my mother sneaked down the back stairwell.

"Where are we going now?" I asked when my father pulled out of the parking structure.

"Logan."

"Thank you, Papa."

"I have filed the flight plan. It's a long trip, Manon. Given you are not cleared to fly, we'll have to break it into two days."

I'd been lost in thought, praying that soon Mantis, Dutch, and I would be back in the States and this all would be just another successful mission. "I'm sorry, what did you say?"

"I know that you're anxious to get to Afghanistan, Manon, but I will not risk fatigue."

"I expected to fly commercial."

He laughed.

"I'm serious. You have to stay with *Maman*."

When I looked between my two parents, their expressions were ones I was very familiar with. The conversation was over, and whatever they said, was the way it was going to be.

Two days later, walking two paces behind my dad and dressed in traditional Afghani attire, I listened as he negotiated a deal with Abdul Ghafor. In exchange for ten million dollars, wired to an offshore account, Ghafor was happy to give Monsieur Mondreau the exact whereabouts of Mantis Cassman along with the details of the arrangement that had been made for the hostage exchange.

The deal my father had made was for the money to become available as soon as he received word that Mantis and Dutch were both on their way back to the United States. Any deviation would result in the money being immediately withdrawn.

Now it was up to me to give Doc a heads-up about the plan my father had put in place.

"*Where in the hell are you?*" Doc bellowed when he answered my call.

"Islamabad."

"You wanna tell me what the fuck you think you're doing?"

"The hostage exchange is due to take place at zero six hundred tomorrow, and I'm requesting backup."

I heard what sounded like Doc dropping the phone, followed by muttering, probably to Razor and Gunner.

"You know you're fired, right?" he said, coming back on the line.

"Yes, sir. Although I am a partner, sir."

"Fill me in, Mondreau, and make it quick."

"I could hear him all the way over here," my father said, smiling.

"Doc Butler doesn't intimidate me."

He raised an eyebrow.

"I just pretend he's you."

He laughed and motioned to a chair near the window. "Come sit with me."

Our room had a spectacular view of the sun setting on Rawal Lake. It was hard to believe that such a beautiful place could be the center of so much turmoil.

"We're in a building constructed in the twenty-first century, yet all around us are people who still live in the dark ages," he said, coming to stand beside me. "I'm very proud of your bravery, Manon."

"You shouldn't be. If this doesn't go right, I'm going to get us all killed."

He narrowed his gaze at me. "Do not lose confidence now, daughter. Your plan is sound. Monsieur Butler should be able to execute it effectively."

I nodded and let out a deep breath. I'd convinced my parents to help me sneak out of a hospital, fly more than halfway around the world, and negotiate a deal worth a great deal of their own money with a known terrorist. Doc Butler should have been the least of my worries, but he wasn't.

54

Dutch

I opened my eyes, wishing I could rub the spot on my head where my captors had pistol-whipped me. It hurt like hell, but it wasn't the only part of my body that did.

I couldn't quite piece together what had happened over the course of the last few days. The last thing I remembered clearly was arriving at Ramstein. What happened after that was murky.

I vaguely remembered being in a hotel with a naked woman, Malin finding me wandering the streets, and then the same men I'd escaped from earlier in the day, bursting into her apartment, taking me hostage for the second time.

I wished I could remember more about Malin's behavior in the short time I'd been with her. Had she acted pissed? Pissed enough to let the men looking for me know she'd taken me in and made me an easy target?

I'd worry she was being held captive like I was, but I remembered someone saying the rest of the apartment was empty.

I could hear voices speaking in what sounded like Pashto, talking about me. The other name I recognized was Mantis. I understood enough of what they were saying to figure out that I was the bait to lure my friend here, and once Mantis arrived, we'd both be dead men.

"Where is Cassman?" Zamed Safi demanded as he had for the last several hours, each time with a different threat as to how I would die if I continued to refuse to answer him.

"As I've told you, I have no idea."

"Are you prepared, then, to die?"

"You won't kill me. But there is something else you could do that would be a lot smarter."

The man looked perplexed. "What?" he finally spat.

I nodded my head at one of the other chairs. "Have a seat. Let's negotiate. Maybe there's a way we can both get what we want."

Before I could continue, I heard shots ring out. The door flew open, and four men clad in tactical gear stormed in.

"Let's get you the fuck outta here," said the man whose voice I recognized as Razor's. As he untied me, I heard more shots fired, and looked over at Zamed's lifeless body.

"That's my handiwork," Razor shouted as he freed my legs. "I told Mantis it was time to end this bloodline."

"I don't think I can walk," I said when I tried to stand and found my legs had little feeling in them.

"Yeah, I know," he answered, motioning toward the other men.

Someone else threw me over his shoulder, probably Doc, and carried me out to one of the two waiting vehicles.

"Fucking amateurs," I heard Doc mutter as he carried me past the dead bodies of every single one of Zamed's men, echoing what I remembered thinking when they had me held captive in Germany.

I'd been able to escape on my own then, but this time, they'd made it harder. If it hadn't been for Razor, Doc, and the rest of the K19 crew, I likely wouldn't have made it out of the hovel they had me hidden in alive.

"Thanks, guys," I said when Doc, Razor, Onyx, and Monk took off their head gear. "You brought in the big guns."

Doc nodded. "Gunner is with Striker, Diesel, and Ranger, trying to save your asshole best friend's life as we speak."

"What did he do?"

"Made a deal with the devil, otherwise known as Abdul Ghafor."

"What was the deal?" I asked, already guessing the answer.

"He's in the midst of offering up his life in exchange for yours."

I groaned. "Have they intercepted him yet?"

Doc shook his head. "No word."

"Where are we?" I asked, looking out of the windows but not seeing any identifiable landmarks. "I hate to admit this, but I don't remember much about the last few days."

"Head injuries will do that, and we're just outside Islamabad."

"Should've figured," I muttered. Only someone as inexperienced as Zamed would take a prisoner to the city he was known to live in. I leaned over to Doc. "I need to ask you about someone."

"Kilbourne?"

"Yeah. Did she turn on me?"

Doc shook his head again. "I can't answer that. We haven't been able to locate her."

"Shit," I muttered, almost wishing she had turned, at least then I'd know she wasn't bound and gagged, fearing for her life like I had been only minutes earlier.

"Doc…"

"I know, Dutch. We're working on it."

I rested my head against the back of the seat and closed my eyes. "It's been one hell of a month," I muttered.

"I'd say."

My eyes flew open and my head popped up. "How's Alegria? Did I dream getting a message from you saying she was in an accident?"

"No, you didn't dream it." Doc scrubbed his face with his hand. "I want to wring her damn neck, but otherwise, she's okay."

I waited for him to go on, but he didn't. "Doc?"

"She's in Islamabad too."

"What? Why?"

"Some crazy fucking idea that she was going to get both you and Mantis all on her own. Once she filled me in on her 'plan,' we came up with one of our own."

"What was her plan?"

"Meeting with Ghafor herself, using our team as backup."

"*Jesus.*"

When Doc's phone vibrated, he pulled it out of his pocket. "They've got him," he said, tossing it on the seat.

"Good to go back to base?" Razor asked.

Doc nodded. "Affirmative."

55

Mantis

After spending two days at a hotel, waiting in limbo for word that the exchange was on, I was summoned downstairs by one of Ghafor's men. Just as I was ushered into the SUV that would transport me to the rendezvous location, the vehicle was surrounded. I was pulled away by men dressed in unfamiliar tactical gear, a bag was thrown over my head, and I was put into a different vehicle.

When the door slammed and the vehicle sped away, someone pulled the bag off.

"We got him," Gunner said into a radio mic.

"*Fuck!*" I shouted. "*Do you realize what you've just done?*"

"Sure do," Gunner answered, not looking at me.

"Dutch is—"

"Just fine, asshole. Like he would've been anyway if you hadn't decided to go rogue and mount your own op."

"Where is he?"

"On his way back to Bagram."

"Are you sure? Who went in after him?"

"Doc."

"On his own?"

"Razor was with him. Monk and Onyx too." Gunner turned his head so I could see his scowl. "Instead of questioning me about whether or not K19 has the best goddamn extraction teams on the planet, you might consider showing some gratitude for the fact that we kept your ass alive."

"Thanks," I said to Ranger, who was driving, Diesel seated in the front passenger seat, and Striker who was seated in the third row behind me. I turned back to Gunner. "I'm sorry, and thank you."

"That's better."

"What about Safi?"

"On his way to hell, along with the rest of the men who had Dutch."

"Any word on Kilbourne?"

"You know about that, huh?"

"Was she in on it?"

"Won't be able to answer that until we find her."

"Which means she may be in trouble too."

"Affirmative. Anyone else you want to ask about?"

"I don't think so."

"What about Alegria? Any idea what she's been up to the last few days?"

I didn't like where Gunner was going with this. "Do you have something to tell me?"

"Seems you weren't the only K19 team member goin' rogue. She and her daddy negotiated a ten-million-dollar payout if Ghafor delivered both you and Dutch."

"Are you fucking kidding me?"

"Can't say I am."

"Where'd the money come from? The agency?"

"Hell no. She pulled this stunt all on her own."

Ten million dollars? Where did she get that kind of money? How had she been able to contact Ghafor to offer the deal in the first place?

"I'm not following. So what happened? Ghafor gave you my twenty?"

"Are you serious? No, Ghafor didn't give us your twenty. Jesus." Gunner glared at me. "I'll ask again, who the fuck do you think you're dealin' with here? We found you all on our own before little Miss Ten Mil and her daddy could make things worse."

"And Dutch?"

"You think Ghafor knew where he was being held? Negative on that one too."

"So where's Ghafor?"

"God knows, but we're on our way to get Alegria and her daddy now."

"What do you mean?"

"They're in Islamabad. I told Doc I don't understand why we had to escort them home; seems like they got here all on their own."

Alegria and her father were in Islamabad? I would ask Gunner if he was sure, but I didn't want to sound like I didn't trust the man or the team's abilities for the third time.

And what about the money? If K19 had intercepted me and picked up Dutch, did that mean Ghafor walked away with Alegria's ten million? Something was telling me it wasn't going to go down quite that easily.

56

Alegria

I watched my father check his phone. There was still no word from Ghafor about where and when the exchange, Mantis for Dutch, was taking place.

The way I'd left things with Doc, he'd agreed to have two teams on standby, one for each man, and the minute I alerted him, they'd move in, while my father and I went back to Bagram Air Base.

It was my father's connection to the *Armée de l'Air Française* that allowed us to land there, not my Air Force or CIA background. He hadn't been willing to share how or why the *Direction générale de la sécurité extérieure* was able to give him such quick and easy access to a man who ultimately, many believed, would come to be as universally hated as Osama bin Laden had been—perhaps even worse.

When Mantis recounted what had happened on his final Afghani mission, he'd told me that he made a deal with Abdul Ghafor in order to gain access to the Taliban and Bagish Safi. He didn't outline the specifics of that deal, but my guess was that there had been a lot of money involved, just like there was now. That, along with Bagish Safi's head on a platter.

I paced, biting my nails like an anxious child rather than an operative who had been down the road of waiting for word countless times.

When we heard someone coming down the hall, both my father and I grabbed our weapons, but not quickly enough.

The cot where I'd been deposited with my hands and feet bound, I estimated, was twenty or thirty feet from where Special Agent Kilbourne was conversing with a man I guessed was a close advisor to Abdul Ghafor.

The first thing I overheard was that two separate K19 teams had successfully extracted Dutch as well as intercepted Mantis and stopped him from offering himself in exchange for Dutch's release. Rather than support my op, Doc had mounted his own. Subsequently, given there was no longer a need for his help, the money my father had negotiated to pay Ghafor for their release had been withdrawn, and I'd been kidnapped instead—most likely in an effort to get the money transfer reinstated.

What I hadn't been able to figure out was what Kilbourne was doing here. Had she been turned and was now working for the Islamic State, or was this all part of a mission designed to infiltrate and bring the organization down? If so, it meant that the agency would know Kilbourne's whereabouts, and as soon as they could make it happen without blowing the operative's cover, I would be rescued.

57

Mantis

Nothing about Alegria's involvement sat right with me. If anyone other than a K19 senior partner had told me she was in Islamabad with her father, I would have been certain we were walking into a trap.

"She and her father are in a suite on the top floor," said Gunner. "You wanna go along or let us handle it?"

Without answering, I opened the door of the SUV when it pulled up to the front of the hotel.

"Wait," said Striker, handing me a protective vest. "Put this on, and we'll be right behind you."

Gunner, Striker, and Diesel followed me inside while Ranger stayed with the vehicle.

The elevator door closed with only me inside; the other three men would separate, each taking a different route to the top floor, as was our standard procedure.

When the elevator door closed behind me, I drew my weapon, knowing nothing was ever as easy as it appeared, particularly when my gut was telling me something was off. The fact that Striker had insisted I wear the bulletproof vest was evidence that he was equally concerned.

I crept down the hallway with my body pressed up against the wall, gun drawn. The fear and anxiety-driven adrenaline felt like a thousand fire ants crawling over my body. When I rounded the corner to where the suite was, I saw its door was open. I made eye contact with both Gunner and Striker, who were approaching from different directions.

Striker got there first and kicked the door the rest of the way in. With guns drawn, we entered the suite. Near the window, we could see Pierre Mondreau, gagged and bound, head slouched, and blood dripping from his scalp. Gunner motioned for me to check Pierre's condition while he systematically checked the other rooms.

"All clear," Gunner announced. "What is his condition?"

"He's alive," I reported as I untied Alegria's father. The man groaned and opened his eyes.

"A woman. Alegria," he muttered before losing consciousness again.

"Call for backup and a bus," I heard Gunner shout.

Abdul Ghafor answered my call on the first ring.

"Ah, if it isn't the little insect calling. What can I do for you, you bastard?"

"What do you want, Abdul? Ten million? It's done."

"Ten? Is that all this pretty little bird is worth to you? Granted, her wings have been clipped, so perhaps she's lost some of her value."

How did Ghafor know Alegria hadn't been cleared to fly? Who in the hell was feeding him information?

"Name your price."

"One hundred million."

I closed my eyes and shook my head. "The United States Government does not negotiate with terrorists nor do they pay ransom," I answered by rote.

"Your government has nothing to do with this. I'll wait for your call. Unless it is to tell me you have my money, don't bother. You have four hours."

"Or?"

"More than the little bird's wings will be clipped."

I set my phone down on the table in front of me. I didn't need to bother telling the men seated around it what Ghafor demanded; they'd all heard what he said.

"I need a minute." I stalked through the sliding door to the patio.

All the miles I'd traveled, all the roads revenge had driven me down since that fateful eleventh day of September, had led me to where I was today.

It was my fault that Ghafor had Alegria. My fault that Dutch had been kidnapped in Germany. My fault that every K19 partner, other than Doc's wife, was in Afghanistan, risking their lives.

I'd heard it said countless times that revenge was like drinking poison and waiting for the other person to die. In this case, the deal I'd made with Ghafor—to gain access to the final man I held personally responsible for my brother's death—had resulted in the people I cared about being forced to drink my poison.

The night I left Alegria in the hospital in Boston, I'd known in my heart that I was prepared to do whatever it took to get Dutch free, including offering my life for his.

I would do the same now, except Ghafor didn't want my life; he wanted money—more money than I'd see in a thousand lifetimes.

58

Dutch

We were less than fifty kilometers from Bagram Air Base when Doc's phone vibrated again. I could tell he really didn't want to look at it, but he slowly picked it up and read the message on the screen.

"*Goddammit. God, motherfucking, dammit.*"

"What?" asked Razor from the front passenger seat.

"They've got Alegria."

"*Who does?*" I demanded.

"*I don't fucking know yet!*"

I watched as Doc punched a code into his phone and waited for someone to pick up his call.

I could overhear Gunner's description of the scene at the Islamabad hotel as well as Alegria's father's report that an American woman had been part of the team that stormed the room and took his daughter.

"Where to, Doc?" Razor asked from the front seat.

"I want everyone back at the base as soon as they can get there."

"But—"

268

"*Save it!*" Doc bellowed. "Everyone back at the base. We have one mission left, and that is to get Alegria back from whoever the motherfucker is who has her, and to get home. That's it. Nothing else. Monk, pull the fuck over."

Smart man, I thought, when Monk pulled the vehicle to the side of the road. I'd known Doc Butler a long time, and I'd never seen him this angry. He probably had been; I'd just never seen him lose control.

Doc got out and opened the front passenger door of the vehicle.

"What?" asked Razor, who was sitting in it.

"You and Dutch start working on a profile for Kilbourne. Let's figure out exactly whose side she's on."

I'd spent the last few days turning that exact question over and over in my head and thinking through every detail of the time we'd been together—before I dumped her for Alegria.

Every time I thought back on that time of my life, I cringed. Had she been more serious about me than I was about her and I just hadn't seen it?

Because of it, had she set me up for easy recapture by Safi out of revenge? And now, had she orchestrated Alegria's kidnapping out of the same revenge?

My instincts were telling me no, she hadn't done any of those things, but in the absence of a better explanation, doubt continued to creep in.

"Kilbourne. Malin. Twenty-six. Graduated first in her class from the University of Virginia. Recruited before graduation. First job was at Langley, but you already know that part." Razor rubbed his chin. "I'm not sure if you want to hear this part."

"What?"

"You were it for her, man."

"What does that mean?"

"Well, you weren't her first, or anything like that, but before you, she hadn't been involved with anyone since high school. No one after you either."

"Fuck," I muttered.

"I don't see it, though."

"What's that?"

"There is a million-mile divide between 'Dutch Miller broke my heart' and 'I'll hook up with the Islamic State and see if I can get my revenge on him that way. And coincidentally, the woman he left me for just happens to be in Islamabad, so what the hell, I'll take her down too.'"

"What's your take, then?" asked Doc.

"We can find out more once we get back to Bagram."

59

Mantis

"Heard from Doc, he wants everyone to meet back at Bagram," said Striker, joining me outside.

I spun around. *"We're abandoning her?"*

Striker grasped my shoulder. "Settle down, man. Of course we aren't abandoning her. We're eliminating risk."

"What about her father?"

"Already on his way."

"What the fuck?"

Striker's grip on my shoulder tightened. "We don't answer to you, Cassman. We make decisions at the time they're needed. Not that you asked, but I'm with Doc on this one. If Alegria and her father had been at Bagram, none of this would be happening."

"Don't blame her."

"Jesus Christ," Striker muttered. "Pull your head out of your ass, Mantis. You aren't making sense. You keep this up, and I'll recommend you get taken off this mission."

"You can't do that."

"Of course I can, and you know it."

I was about to say I'd go it alone then, but that was the point Striker was trying to make. The fact that I and then Alegria had gone it alone, was what turned everything into a clusterfuck in the first place. Even Dutch had to a certain extent. If he'd communicated, the way he was supposed to, we'd all probably be back in the States right now.

"I hear you," I conceded.

"Good. Now let's move."

When we returned to Bagram, Dutch, Doc, and the rest of that crew were already back, but I'd only seen Doc and Monk.

"Where's Dutch?" I asked.

"He and Razor are working on a profile of Kilbourne."

"Do you think she's the one who set up Alegria?"

"Only logical explanation at this point. There's no intel indicating another American woman's involvement," said Doc.

I went in search of Dutch and found him with Striker and Razor, and Striker was doing all the talking. I rapped on the window, and Razor motioned me in.

"Hey, man," I said to Dutch, who stood, and we hugged, thumping each other hard on the back. "Damn good to see you."

"Same here, you jackass."

I laughed. "I try to save your sorry ass, and you call me names," I joked. "Seriously though, thanks for ending the Safi bloodline."

"You can thank him," said Dutch, pointing at Razor. "He was a man on a mission as far as taking Zamed out."

"Bastards, all of 'em," muttered Razor. He and Striker looked like they were waiting for me to leave so they could get back to whatever they had been talking about before I came in.

"I'll catch up with you later."

"Where're you goin'?" asked Razor, pointing to a chair. "Sit your ass down here."

"Didn't want to interrupt."

"Striker's briefing us on Kilbourne's mission."

My eyes opened wider. "What is it?"

"The Pakistani Taliban began recruiting women in the middle of last year. The Islamic State, as hard as it is for them to accept women as human beings, is realizing that for them to keep their dwindling numbers up, they're going to have to do the same thing."

I'd heard about the recruitment tactics encouraging women to spread a fundamentalist message and support holy war. The idea that they could be trained to keep a pistol and a grenade, while supporting their husbands and promoting and living the teachings of the prophet Muhammad, had them signing up in droves.

"Kilbourne has been recruited as a trainer," said Striker. "We don't know whether she set Dutch up for recapture, but it seems likely as a means to prove her loyalty."

"Exactly what I thought about her facilitating Alegria's kidnapping," added Razor. "If she had refused, she'd be dead. Doing anything other than what they asked of her would not only blow her cover, it would end her life."

"Do you think it's personal?" asked Dutch.

"Not remotely so," answered Striker. "In fact, I think she would've walked away from you if you hadn't ended your relationship with her when you did. This mission has been in the works for well over a year. She was scheduled to leave shortly after Mantis did."

"Huh," responded Dutch, scratching his chin.

"You're not the Casanova you thought you were," taunted Razor.

"What's next, then?" I asked.

"We go get Alegria the hell out of there," Razor answered.

"Who's on the team?" I prayed Razor would include me. Sitting here, powerless to help rescue the woman I loved, would drive me insane. If anything went wrong, God forbid, I'd forever blame myself.

Razor looked back and forth between Dutch and me. "I want both of you on this, but I have to know you're committed—"

"Committed? Hell, we—"

"Jesus Christ," said Striker to Dutch. "You're as bad as Mantis. Shut the fuck up and listen to what Razor has to say."

"Don't question my commitment. *Not fucking ever.*"

I wished I could tell Dutch to shut the hell up too, and in any other circumstance, I probably would have. This was textbook for my best friend.

"This is fun, girls, but I need to get this op set up. So, what I was going to say was I need to know that you're committed to going in to get Alegria, but leaving Kilbourne to complete her mission. She's worked damn hard to infiltrate this organization."

"Meaning what, exactly?" I asked.

"She knows enough to stay out of the way. Keep her safe, but make it look unintentional."

I could read the way Dutch was processing what Razor had just said. It would be difficult for him to execute the op in that way. His instinct would be to get both Alegria and Malin out of the hands of the Islamic

State, but as Striker said, Malin had spent months putting this op together, likely at great cost to the agency. K19 would find themselves in a huge shitstorm if they didn't agree to the terms of this extraction.

"What was she doing in Germany?" Dutch asked.

"Finding you, although not for the CIA; for Safi."

"I thought she was working for Ghafor."

"She is."

Knowing Ghafor as well as I did, it stood to reason he saw that using her to get Dutch would serve a purpose unrelated to the recruitment of women soldiers. Taking out Zamed would have also been high on Abdul's list of priorities.

"The agency will only give us Ghafor's twenty if we ensure that whoever tries to interfere will be taken out."

"Taken out? What the fuck?"

"That's how serious they are, Dutch," said Razor. "Those are our orders."

"Who else is going in?" I asked.

"Just the four of us."

"So which one of you is gonna handle the kill if I screw up?" Dutch laughed.

"We'll let Mantis do it," Razor answered, and he didn't sound like he was kidding.

60

Alegria

I couldn't say why, but I knew Kilbourne was working an op. There was nothing the woman had done to give me any indication she was, but my instincts filled in the blanks.

As far as my treatment, my accommodations weren't the best, but no one roughed me up. It made sense given Ghafor didn't want information, but my father's money. I wasn't naive enough to think that once he had it I'd be released. I'd seen his vulnerabilities, and that was something he wouldn't want the world—his enemies in particular—to know.

He was way short on cash, his arsenal was almost depleted, and anyone who knew anything about the Islamic State would know that the only reason they would ever consider recruiting women was if the number of their foot soldiers was low enough to threaten the organization's existence.

If I was going to survive this, I had to figure out a way to escape.

"Who is that?" I heard a man ask with what I guess was a Russian accent. I couldn't see him from where I was bound and gagged, but something about his voice sounded familiar.

Russian influence with the Islamic State had traditionally been limited to Syria, at least publicly. Who and what they supported behind the veil of covert black ops could be virtually anyone's guess.

"Ah, if it isn't the beautiful Alegria," said the man who had been rumored dead, and then rumored alive again—Sergei Orlov. His being here didn't necessarily mean Russian involvement, however. Orlov, known in intelligence circles as *Oruzhiye* or the Gun, contracted with the highest bidder.

Sergei walked over, removed the gag, and stroked a finger down my cheek. "I'd heard you were shot."

I backed away from his touch. "What are you doing here, Orlov?"

He smiled. "There are any number of reasons I might be here, Miss Mondreau. Any number."

Out of the corner of my eye, I caught Malin watching us. She quickly recovered, but not quickly enough. I wondered if I was the only one who saw it—Orlov being here was somehow a direct threat to Agent Kilbourne.

61

Mantis

"We're in," Striker told Dutch and me. "We'll head out at twenty-one hundred."

I nodded. I'd hoped to have more time to talk to Dutch, but it would have to wait; we were leaving in fifteen minutes.

"Who in the hell is that?" Razor asked. "Jesus, what the fuck is Orlov doing here?"

I looked in the direction that Razor was pointing, and watched as Sergei Orlov, paid assassin, touched Alegria's face. I took a deep breath, knowing I had to wait for Razor's signal, but right now, I wanted to storm in and rip Orlov's arm off. His being here was definitely a complication we hadn't anticipated.

"Shit," I heard Striker mutter. He'd gone around and scoped out where we might be able to go in on the side of the building, and was just now seeing Orlov. "What is he doing here?"

"Who?" asked Dutch, who walked up with Striker.

"*Oruzhiye.*"

"What's he doing here?"

"That's four for four, gentlemen. No one knows why he's here, and worse, no one knows what to do about it."

"Alegria is our target," I said. "We go in. We get her. We get out. If we aren't supposed to upset Kilbourne's op, then we can't go in there and shoot up the place."

"You should know that Alegria's father agreed to pay whatever Ghafor wants," said Striker.

"A hundred million bucks? Are you kidding me? Did you know her family had that kind of money?" Dutch asked me. I shook my head.

"I don't think Alegria knew."

"Her family is pretty weird."

"Her mother has stage-four pancreatic cancer."

"Shit," murmured Dutch. "Now I feel like an asshole."

"That's because you are an asshole," said Razor. "Now shut up so I can think this through."

"We should wait it out until Orlov leaves," suggested Striker.

I thought the edict from the agency was bullshit. We should be able to go in, get Alegria, and whatever casualties there were would be collateral damage. As far as I was concerned, as long as we were here, we should pull Malin Kilbourne out too. What the hell? Why not take out Ghafor and Orlov while we were at it, and rid the world of two more wastes of flesh?

Would the Islamic State be able to endure without Ghafor? I doubted it. Al-Qaeda was far less of a threat once bin Laden was assassinated. They struggled along, raised their ugly monster heads from time to time, but were they considered the biggest threat to the United States? Hardly.

"What're you thinking?" asked Razor.

"You don't wanna know."

I should've known that was the absolute wrong thing to say to Razor Sharp. "I sure do," he said, smirking.

"I don't give a shit about what the agency wants. One of our own is inside, and we need to get her out."

"So you don't want to wait."

"Hell, no."

"And Orlov?"

"Good excuse as ever to take out that *sonuvabitch*."

"If Doc was with us, Orlov would already be dead. Same for Gunner. He'd kill the man with his bare hands."

Back when the world thought they were finally rid of *Oruzhiye*, he'd taken Doc's now wife, Merrigan, hostage, and used her to attempt to gain the upper hand with Moscow's current ruling party, United Russia. Only believing he was already dead had stopped Doc from hunting him down and making sure he had a very slow and very painful end of life.

Orlov had turned up again when United Russia put out a hit on Gunner's soon-to-be wife's head. Zary, who had also been a Russian assassin, had defected and had asked Gunner to help her. Gunner would want Orlov dead in the same way Doc would.

No matter who was here or wasn't, just about everyone who had ever worked in intelligence would celebrate the "second death" of the bastard.

"Let's kill him," said Razor, looking from me to Dutch to Striker. "The agency said we couldn't jeopardize Kilbourne's mission. They didn't say a word about not killing Orlov."

"Because they didn't expect him to be here," said Striker.

"Screw 'em."

"Does that mean we can extract Kilbourne too?" asked Dutch.

Razor looked at Striker.

"How hard do you want to bite the hand that feeds you?" Striker asked.

"What are they gonna do, fire us?" answered Razor.

"You might not get any more assignments."

"Assignments? Hell, who wants 'em anyway? We've all been talkin' about retiring."

I watched Striker's reaction. He was probably the only one of the new partners who hadn't been privately contracting for years. It wasn't as though he couldn't start if K19 folded. The odds of that were pretty damn slim. The men and women who made up the team were the best in the world, and the agency knew it.

My head spun around when I heard Dutch's bird call. What the fuck did he think he was doing? He'd just forced their hand. Alegria would know they were close, and if we waited even an hour to move in, she'd probably try to escape on her own and get herself killed. There was a reason Orlov was there, and while I didn't know what it was, I didn't doubt for a minute that he'd been sent to kill someone.

"You bastard," I heard Striker seethe. "What do you think you're doing?" Striker had Dutch by the throat, and before I could move in and separate them, Razor did. He pushed Striker back and stayed in front of Dutch.

"This isn't your op, Ellis. You'd do well to remember who you work for."

Out of the four of us, I should've been the one with the least level head, given the love of my life was being held hostage by a jihadist madman, but in this case, I wasn't.

"Stand down, all three of you. If you can't get it together, then I'll go in on my own." I wanted to add that I'd prefer it that way, but then I'd be just as bad as they were.

62

Alegria

I heard Dutch's signal, but worse, Kilbourne did too. What happened next would confirm exactly who Malin was working for. If she acted, it would mean she'd been turned. If she ignored it, she was working an op. I held my breath and waited, but the agent didn't show any sign of acknowledgment.

I looked from Kilbourne to Orlov, and my blood ran cold. He'd heard it too, recognized it, and all hell was about to break loose.

In the same moment Orlov grabbed Malin and put a gun to her head, Dutch, Mantis, Striker, and Razor stormed the room. It didn't look like they'd thrown smoke grenades in the small space, more likely smoke bombs, and only enough to hide my extraction.

Mantis rushed over, threw me over his shoulder, and was out before enough of the smoke had cleared for anyone to have visibility across the room.

We were in the back of the SUV, and Mantis had me untied before I could've counted to ten. Seconds later, Razor and Striker climbed in the front.

"Where the fuck is Dutch?" Striker yelled. "That motherfuck—"

"There he is," said Razor, pointing to where Orlov was taking Kilbourne out of the building.

"It's an op!" I yelled. *"Go get her."*

I watched as Razor and Striker made eye contact. When Ellis nodded, they both climbed out of the vehicle. Razor tossed Mantis the keys. "Get her the hell out of here."

Mantis climbed over the seat and sped away from the scene.

"What are you doing?" I shouted. *"You can't leave! They're going to—"*

"Reinforcements are on their way. They'll be fine."

"But—"

"Alegria!" he yelled back. *"This was the plan. Now stop."*

When we were several miles from the compound where I had been held, Mantis pulled the vehicle to the side of the road, got out, and opened the back passenger door. "Come here," he said, and I climbed out.

He pushed me up against the side of the SUV, grasped the back of my neck, and covered my mouth with his.

I threw my arms around him, kissing him back so hard it hurt. Our tongues warred against each other, and I heard Mantis growl.

"I love you so fucking much." He put his hands on my bottom and lifted me up until my legs encircled his waist. "Never again, Flygirl."

"Never what?"

"I'm never letting you out of my sight again."

"Mantis—"

"Say my name."

"What do you mean?"

"Tell me you love me, Manon, and say my name."

"I love you, Gehring."

"Forever?"

"Forever."

"I've learned something important in the last year." I smiled. "What's that?"

"I don't want to live this life without you beside me."

"Mantis—"

"Say my name."

I leaned forward and kissed him. "Gehring, I don't want to live my life without you by my side either, although there may be times we have to be out of each other's sight."

"Says who?"

"Doc, for one."

"Screw him. We'll quit."

I shook my head and brought my mouth to his again. "Kiss me," I murmured. "Kiss me hard."

Mantis kept me pinned between him and the SUV, our mouths grinding against each other's until we saw the lights of another vehicle in the distance.

63

Dutch

My eyes met Malin's in the split second between storming the building and throwing the smoke bombs.

She was imploring me with those beautiful hazel eyes, and I was powerless to ignore her and follow the terms of the mission when Orlov had a gun to her head.

I knew Mantis had already extracted Alegria, and the next step should've been for me, Razor, and Striker to exit the building before the men guarding her could see well enough to start shooting.

Orlov also knew time was short before he'd face the same response from Ghafor's guards, especially given he was trying to kidnap a woman they believed worked for their boss.

Speaking of their boss, there had been no sign of Abdul Ghafor.

I made my way through the smoke-filled room, almost not caring who I came in contact with; my weapon was at the ready, and there was no question that I'd shoot first.

"Let her go, Sergei," I said, once we were outside. "She has no value to you."

"On the contrary, it is you to whom she has no value. First you cast her aside to take another man's woman, and then you rescue the same woman with no intention of taking our beautiful Malin with you."

I kept my eyes laser-focused on Orlov, all the while trying to process what he was saying. The Russian knew too much about my history with Malin for this to be a random act. He was here specifically for her, but why?

Striker would know if United Russia had an issue with her involvement with the Islamic State, which seemed highly unlikely, but what other reason could there be?

"What do you want from her, Orlov?" Razor shouted from behind me. "Whatever UR is paying you, we'll double."

When Sergei laughed, I broke my stare and looked at Malin. She was scared, which had to mean she knew why Orlov had his gun at her temple, that he'd come specifically for her, and whatever it was, he'd either kill her or deliver her to whomever was paying him, where she'd eventually meet the same fate.

Each of the K19 partners brought their own special skill set to the table. For me, it was my ability to make the one-in-a-million shot every time I fired. Orlov knew it too. While he may be known as "the Gun," I could very well have been known as "the Sniper."

The truth was, I'd been waiting for this opportunity. Orlov wasn't the only name on my hit list, not by far, but one by one, I intended to pick off every one of them, even if it took me until my last breath to do it.

Time to meet your maker, Sergei.

With Razor and Striker at my back, I didn't hesitate. I fired and hit Orlov right between the eyes before the man knew the shot had gone off.

I ran forward to grab Malin and get her away from the scene, when out of the corner of my eye, I saw Ghafor walking toward us.

64

Mantis

"Papa," Alegria cried.

I stood near the door of the infirmary, watching her reunion with the man who had rarely been there for her when she was growing up.

The disparity between my own upbringing and hers was glaring, yet the love that passed between parent and child was almost universal.

As I watched, I saw no recrimination on her part, only palpable relief that her "Papa" was alive and would make a full recovery from the beatings that had been inflicted on him.

Pierre Mondreau cupped his daughter's face with his hand. "I was so worried about you. Thank God you're safe."

"Look at what they did to you, and it's all my fault."

"*Non, ma fille.*" Her father shook his head.

Alegria turned and looked at me. "We can leave as soon as your father is cleared to travel."

"Thank you," she mouthed and then turned back to her father. "Have you seen the doctor tonight?"

He shook his head.

"Let me see if I can track him down," I offered.

An infirmary on a military base was a little different than a regular hospital. I should be able to find a doctor, and if not, one would come if called.

"How's Alegria doing?" asked Doc, coming toward me from the bank of elevators.

"Shaken, but more worried about her father than herself."

Doc smiled. "Wouldn't expect anything different from Alegria."

"As you can imagine, they're both anxious to get back to Boston."

"I heard her mother is quite ill."

I nodded. "I thought I'd see if I could find a doctor..."

"Will a physician's assistant do?"

"If you can make the decision about whether Pierre can travel, then sure."

Doc picked up the chart he saw sitting on the desk in the nurse's station and read it over. "I think he'll be fine to travel as long as I'm on board with you."

"How many planes do we have here anyway?"

"What do you mean?"

"How did Pierre and Alegria get here?"

Doc shrugged. "Regardless, we have enough pilots to get us back. Excuse me," he said when his phone buzzed.

When I turned to walk away, Doc motioned for me to stay.

"Say that again," I heard him say. "Roger that. Mantis is here. I'll discuss this with him and get back to you."

"That was Razor. There's a situation back in Islamabad. Orlov is dead."

I raised a brow.

"Dutch took the shot."

"Then, he's really dead."

Doc nodded. "Striker is making a deal with Ghafor as we speak."

"What's the deal?"

"They're bringing Kilbourne back. Naturally, Abdul wants something in exchange."

"What?"

"My guess is money."

"Is he really in a position to ask for anything?"

"You know him better than the rest of us do. What's his threat level?"

"To the world?"

"Is there any reason whatsoever to negotiate with him?"

"He was the means to an end for me. If you're asking if I think they should take him out given the opportunity, I'd do it myself if I could be in two places at once."

"Let's get this done, get the hell out of the dark ages, and go home."

I knew exactly what Doc meant. No matter whether world leaders believed there was a war worth waging in this part of the world, nothing could change the fact that the conflicts in the Middle East went back as far as time. It would never matter who invested what kind of money in Afghanistan; a few years and a few billion dollars couldn't rewrite the history of a thousand years.

65

Alegria

"Did you find out anything about my father being able to leave?"

"I did. Doc will fly back to the States with us. There are a handful of details to be worked out, and then we'll all be on our way."

"I see," I answered, looking at my father, who was drifting off to sleep. "Come with me."

I led Mantis down the hallway until I found an open room. "Tell me what's going on."

"I don't know all the details, but evidently Orlov is dead, and Ghafor wants to make a deal."

"For what?"

"To let Malin go, from what I could gather. Doc didn't relay a lot of information."

"He's finished."

"What do you mean? Ghafor?"

"That's right. The Islamic State is barely holding on to a semblance of relevance. My guess is the reason Orlov was there was because Abdul was trying to negotiate with United Russia."

"What would United Russia want from Ghafor?"

"I'm not certain, but I got the feeling that Kilbourne was somehow involved."

"There's a reason UR wants her."

"I agree."

"I told Doc that if it were my decision, we'd take Ghafor out at the first opportunity."

"I would make the same call."

66

Mantis

When we walked back out into the hallway, Doc was waiting.

"It didn't go down quite as we thought it would, but Razor and Dutch are on their way back here with Kilbourne, while Striker, Ranger, and Diesel are working out a deal with Ghafor. My understanding is that they'll be transporting Abdul to a safe house to finalize negotiations."

"It must be something big," said Alegria.

Doc nodded and put his arm around her shoulders. "I sure as hell wanted to wring your neck, but I'm glad you're back with us and safe."

"I just want to go home," she told him.

"You and me both, sweetheart."

67

Dutch

Striker had something big on Ghafor; that would be the only explanation for the Islamic State's leader to fold as easily as he did.

I didn't care what it was, as long as Razor, Malin, and I could get the hell out of there. Once we were back at Bagram, Special Agent Kilbourne and I were going to have a long damn talk about Sergei Orlov. I intended to get to the bottom of who had paid him to hunt her down and why.

Striker didn't seem to have any idea, and if anyone would know, he would.

"The helicopter will be here in ten," said Razor. "We'll take the SUV back to Bagram."

"This way," I said to Malin, who looked at Razor.

"I'll be right behind you," he told her, shooting me a questioning look when she turned her back.

I shrugged and followed her to the SUV.

"I'm not angry," I said when I opened the door for her to climb in. "If you had anything to do with Safi taking me from the apartment, I know you didn't have any choice."

"I did."

"What do you mean?"

"I had a choice."

"We'll discuss this later," I said when I saw Razor approach. "Get in." I motioned to the back passenger door.

"Something's up," Razor said after I closed the door behind her. "Why don't you ride in the back with her?"

"Roger that." I walked to the other side of the vehicle while Razor stood where he was.

"We're going straight to the airfield," Razor said when we arrived at Bagram, glancing over the seat at me. "Onyx will arrange for transport."

I had no idea where Malin and I were going, but wherever it was, Razor didn't want her to know either.

68

Mantis

"You have no idea where he is?" Alegria asked.

I shook my head. "He and Kilbourne left Bagram before we did. All I know is that Onyx was responsible for their transport and that the agency provided another pilot to travel with them."

When Doc gave the word that Alegria's father could be discharged, we were in the air less than two hours later, along with the rest of the K19 crew—minus Striker, Ranger, and Diesel. No one talked about what went down with Ghafor. No one talked about what went down with Dutch and Malin. When we landed at Logan, I asked Doc about Dutch right before we got off the plane.

"There's nothing I can tell you," Doc answered, grasping my shoulder. "You and Alegria take some time. When you're ready to talk about the K19 partnership, let me know."

"Roger that," I said, following Alegria and her father off the plane and into the SUV waiting for us on the tarmac.

"I've made arrangements for an apartment for you near the hospital so you can spend more time with your *maman*," Pierre said to Alegria.

"Would it be better if we went to a hotel for tonight, Papa?" she asked.

He shook his head. "No, your mother is there now."

Alegria rested her head on my shoulder. "Will you stay?" she whispered.

"As long as you're in Boston, that's where I'll be too," I answered, kissing her forehead.

"I'll take your bag; you go see your mother," I told Alegria when Pierre handed me the key card for the second apartment.

"I'll help and join you shortly," Pierre offered.

I was about to tell him I could handle it, but when our eyes met, I realized Pierre wanted to talk to me more than help me.

"I know the time has long since passed that I should ask what your intentions are with my daughter, but I am anyway."

I smiled. "I've loved Manon for all of my adult life."

Pierre raised a brow.

I laughed. "I know I didn't answer your question."

"There was a reason your relationship didn't work in the past."

"Yes, sir."

Pierre folded his arms, and I laughed again.

"How much time ya got?"

Alegria's father sat down in one of the furnished apartment's chairs. "All day."

That certainly wasn't what I'd expected him to say, but the reasons for the decision that had resulted in Alegria ending our relationship weren't a secret.

"My brother was a firefighter for New York City Fire Department," I began.

"I was wondering what happened to the two of you," Alegria commented when her dad and I joined her and her mother.

"How are you feeling, ma'am?" I asked, unsure of whether I should embrace her or offer to shake her hand.

Matille stood to approach me, and I met her half-way, kissing both cheeks when she initiated our embrace.

"Better now that my husband and daughter are here."

"Yes, ma'am," I murmured, wondering if she blamed me for them leaving in the first place.

"*Maman* has good news," Alegria said, putting her arm through mine.

"I'm in a remission of sorts," Matille said to her husband, who put his hands on his wife's shoulders.

"What does this mean?"

I listened as Matille and Alegria rattled off numbers and acronyms that didn't mean anything to me. Even if they had, the conversation I'd had with Pierre was at the forefront of my mind.

"It means the cancer is no longer growing."

Alegria explained that the cancer center where her mother was being treated had recently implemented two experimental therapies from the Netherlands that had promising results.

The four-drug chemo "cocktail" had extended patients' lives by nearly two years over the current, standard single-drug regimen for pancreatic cancer.

"This is very good news," murmured Alegria.

"Next week, they'll begin a combination of chemo with radiation," added Matille.

I wasn't sure what to say. Congratulations, you get to live two years longer than you previously thought?

"What I want to know now is when the two of you plan to get married. I would like as much time with my grandchildren as possible," Matille said with her hands on her hips.

"*Maman*!" gasped Alegria.

Pierre's eyes met mine, and we both smiled.

69

Alegria

"I'm sorry about what my mother said," I muttered, motioning Mantis from the room.

"Don't be." He smiled and drew me close. "Do you think your parents might want some time alone?"

"Probably."

"Because I know I would."

I could feel my cheeks turn pink and my heart rate speed up. There was nothing stopping us from making love. Whether I'd been able to talk to Dutch about it or not, I knew he understood that our relationship was over. In fact, I wondered if maybe he and Malin were rekindling their romance.

"What are you thinking about?" Mantis asked, smiling.

"Being alone with you."

"Good."

We said goodbye to my parents, agreeing to meet up later for dinner.

"Where is the apartment?" I asked when we walked out into the hallway.

"On the fifth floor."

I couldn't explain why, but knowing we were staying on a different floor made me feel less uncomfortable about what we were about to do.

Mantis held my hand while we waited for the elevator, but as soon as it opened, he pushed me up against the back wall and kissed me.

It was a kiss much like the one we'd shared on the side of the road on our way back to Bagram Air Base. It was so hard, it almost hurt as our tongues explored each other's mouths.

"I've never wanted anything more than I want to make love to you right now, Manon."

"I want the same thing," I breathed.

When the elevator opened on our floor, Mantis picked me up and carried me the rest of the way to the apartment door.

"Where is the key?" I asked, not wanting him to put me down.

"The card is in my shirt pocket."

I pulled it out and waved it in front of the door handle. When it clicked, I opened it.

He kissed me again and continued carrying me down the hallway. When we got to the bedroom, Mantis set me on my feet.

"I need to see you naked, baby. Take off your clothes."

I almost swooned. This was what I craved—Mantis taking charge—because I knew what came next would be him bringing pleasure to my body like no one else could.

"Look at you," he groaned. "You take my breath away."

He left me standing where I was, his eyes wandering over every inch of my body. When he'd looked his fill, he came and knelt before me.

"You have too many clothes on," I murmured, getting only a raised eyebrow in response.

Mantis ran his lips across my hips and licked down from my belly button to my pussy. I twined my fingers in his hair.

"It's too much," I groaned. "Please, Mantis. I need you so much."

"Say my name."

"Gehring...please...I need you."

Mantis ran his hands up my legs to my waist, and stood. He walked me backwards to the bed, and I fell into it.

"Hands above your head. Don't move," he warned. "Wait."

Mantis looked into my eyes.

"Nothing between us, Gehring."

He nodded, undressed, and knelt on the bed. "Open for me, Manon." He moved forward so his hardness rested against me.

I let my eyes drift closed, wanting to just feel.

"Look at me," he said. "I love you, Manon. I've never loved anyone other than you."

"I love you, Gehring. I've never loved anyone other than you."

"I want everything with you. Not just to spend my life following wherever you lead..."

I smiled.

"I want you to be my wife, the mother of my children, and the person whose eyes I look into when I wake up in the morning and right before I go to sleep at night. Tell me you want the same thing."

"I do, Gehring. More than anything."

"Tell me you'll marry me."

"I'll marry you."

"And make beautiful babies with me."

My eyes filled with tears, but I was smiling. "Can we start working on that as soon as possible? You know, like now?"

"We can," he answered, easing into me. "God, you feel so good, Manon."

I arched, wanting to feel him deeper.

There was nothing like feeling my body joined together with his. We were a perfect fit. Two halves becoming whole. Two hearts joining together in the same way our bodies did. As he thrust inside me, bringing me closer to the crest of exquisite ecstasy, I prayed that tonight that miracle would happen—that we would make a child that would be from both of our bodies.

I looked into Mantis' eyes and saw as much love in them as I was feeling. I knew we'd be together for the rest of our lives. Just like my parents and his, we'd raise a family and grow old together, and no matter what, we'd stay together, supporting one another regardless of the curveballs life threw us. Wherever one went, the other would follow. Together forever.

70

Mantis

"Don't go anywhere," I said to her again, only this time, I was leaving her sated and sleepy.

She rolled to her side, and I covered her body with the blanket. "You don't go anywhere," she murmured.

I leaned down and kissed her. "I'll be right back."

While my proposal wasn't traditional in that I hadn't gotten down on one knee and presented an engagement ring to Alegria, asking her to marry me in the moments before I slid inside her warmth, was perfect. I hoped she felt the same way.

I crawled in bed next to her, and she snuggled her warm body up against mine.

"What time is it?" she murmured.

"We have a couple of hours before we have to meet your parents."

"We could cancel."

I smiled. "We have a lifetime ahead of us, Manon."

"I know. I've just missed you so much."

I could feel the wetness of her tears on my chest. "Don't cry, baby. We're together now."

She lifted her head and looked into my eyes. "I'm sorry, Gehring. I'm sorry I asked you to choose. I was wrong to do that."

"I'm sorry I put you in that position."

"I want you to know that I understand now. I know you didn't have a choice."

"Thank you," I said, just above a whisper, willing my own tears to stay at bay. I'd mourn my brother for the rest of my life, and I'd still fight against the forces of evil that threatened the lives of the people I cared about, but now, Alegria and I would do it side by side.

71

Alegria

I couldn't name which part of my life made me happiest tonight. Knowing Mantis and I would one day be married and spend our lives together, or that my mother had such promising news about her cancer treatment, or that my father and I had bonded in a way I'd never dreamed we would.

He sat across from me now, at dinner, looking at me with such pride that I felt as though my heart would burst. I'd wanted to see that look in his eyes all of my life. And now, there it was. Every time my father looked at me, I knew he loved me.

Mantis brought my hand to his lips. "I love you, Manon. Do you know how much?"

"I do."

He let go and pushed his chair back from the table. "Are you sure you know how much?"

I watched as he knelt next to me, took my hand in his, and pulled a small box out of his jacket pocket.

"If you ever doubt my love for you, I want you to look at the ring I'm about to put on your finger, and know that I love you with every cell of my body, my whole heart, every breath I take."

"I know," I whispered as he slid the ring on my finger.

Mantis leaned forward. "You still want to marry me, right?" he whispered.

"Yes!" I shouted. "Yes, I want to marry you."

I could hear my parents murmuring congratulations, maybe even other people in the restaurant offering theirs too, but none of it mattered. Listening to Mantis tell me he loved me was all I wanted to hear, not just now, but for the rest of my life.

72

Mantis

We rode the elevator with Pierre and Matille, saying good night when they got off on the second floor.

"There's something I need to show you," I said to Alegria, pulling my phone out of my pocket. "I received this on our way back from the restaurant."

I held the phone out to her.

"What is it?"

I smiled as she read the text that had come through from the man who had been my best friend and hers since our days at the Air Force Academy.

Don't you worry. The best man will be back in time for the wedding. Congratulations, and I love you both.

EPILOGUE

Mantis

"You bought one!" exclaimed Alegria when her father led her, Matille, and me out on the tarmac. "Wait. That's K19's plane."

Pierre shrugged. "I made your friend an offer he couldn't refuse. The delivery delay for a Cirrus Vision is presently over twenty-four months long."

Alegria's father winked at me, since I'd been the one to finally convince Doc to sell the Vision to him.

When Pierre apologized, saying he wanted to be the one to fly with Alegria as she piloted her first flight since she'd been shot, I hadn't minded.

Instead, I focused back to the day, years ago, when Manon Mondreau, now Manon Cassman, took her first solo flight. The look on her face then was one I'd never forgotten and never would.

Matille and I waited in the SUV until we saw the plane approaching the runway to land. Bottle of champagne in hand, I stood and watched them taxi in until I finally saw the door open, and my beautiful wife climb out of the plane.

I popped the cork and poured the bottle's contents over both of us as I held her in my arms.

She laughed and laughed, just like she had the day I'd given her her call sign.

"I love you so much, Mrs. Cassman."

"And I love you, Mr. Cassman."

I rested my hand on her belly and caressed the bump I felt there.

"Ian's first flight," she beamed.

I smiled too, not arguing about whether we were having a boy or a girl. Nor did I argue about the name she'd chosen for our baby if we had a boy.

Everything I'd thought I'd lost, I'd won again, and I was the happiest man alive.

Keep reading for a sneak peek
at the next book
in the K19 Security Solutions
series—
DUTCH!

1

Dutch

Her skin was tan from the sun, and her lips were ruby red. Her shoulder-length inky-black hair was the same color as the thin silk camisole she wore to stave off the heat. When its spaghetti strap slid off her shoulder, I couldn't help but wind it around my finger and pull it just a little lower, causing her to try to shrug away and shoot me a look of confusion.

Up until five o'clock today, I wouldn't have laid a hand on her. Now, all bets were off. I was no longer Special Agent Malin "Starling" Kilbourne's boss. In fact, I no longer worked for the CIA at all, which meant I intended to start fulfilling every fantasy I'd had about the woman who made my blood run hot.

Malin covered my hand with hers. "What are you doing?"

I smiled. "Peeking."

I watched as she looked past me, searching the crowded outdoor patio for the rest of the team that had gone out to celebrate both the end of a mission and my leaving the agency. When her gaze settled on me and she moved her hand away, I took the opportunity to walk her backwards a few short steps until she rested against the cool stone wall of the building.

Her look challenged more than questioned, and when I leaned in to run my tongue along her clavicle, sweet Miss Malin gasped and closed her eyes.

Was she surprised? Had she not seen this coming? Hadn't she felt how the air around us crackled when I got within a foot of her?

I was done denying myself the knowledge of how her naked body would feel under mine. I pulled the camisole a little lower until I could see the tip of her dusty-rose nipple.

—Malin—

It wasn't just the heat and humidity of the summer night that made it hard for me to breathe; Thomas "Dutch" Miller, my former boss as of a few short hours ago and star of every fantasy I'd had as a woman, had his hands on me. Not just his hands, his lips and tongue too.

I was used to seeing him in the dark suits he wore to work every day along with a crisp, white button-down shirt and a conservative tie. Tonight, he wore a faded blue t-shirt that was the perfect size to show off the muscles I knew he worked hard to maintain and a pair of khaki cargo shorts. His blond hair was cropped close, but I'd heard him say he intended to grow it long now that he was retiring—at least from working directly for the agency. I'd also heard that he planned to join a private firm owned by several former agency operatives.

As much as I wanted to watch as he bent his head and laved the nipple he'd just exposed, my eyes drifted closed. With one hand, I clutched his arm, not to stop him, but in an attempt to hang on for dear life as the man set my already overheated body on fire.

I was disappointed when he drew the strap of my camisole back up to my shoulder, but groaned with equal intensity when he pulled my arm away from my body and studied the tattoo on the soft skin covering my tricep. He leaned forward again and ran the hard tip of his tongue over the right arrow, the one with the shaft piercing a diamond. That one symbolized invincibility. He moved to the left, tracing the feathered arrow that represented liberty, triumph, and independence.

"I like these," he murmured, raising his head so his lips were close enough to mine to touch. "I like them on your skin."

If I could speak, I wouldn't know what to say. The man had equally intimidated and excited me since the day the CIA's human resource officer led me into his office.

"You're mine now, Kilbourne," Dutch had said that day, but not meaning it in the way I'd wanted him to even after a few minutes in his presence.

Part of me had considered asking for a different assignment, but I didn't. Doing so would've been more of a career-killer than lusting after my first boss.

I put both hands under his shirt and rested my palms just above the waist of his shorts. His skin was hot to the touch while mine alternated between scorching and covered in chill bumps depending on where he ran his tongue.

"You're mine now, Malin," he murmured, his words fulfilling the first fantasy I'd had of what it would be like to be seduced by him. "Let's get out of here."

He took my hand and led me out the back gate of the bar's patio and to his car. He pushed me up against the passenger door and rested his rock-hard body flush with mine.

"Tell me you want this as much as I do," he said, his eyes boring into mine.

"I do," I breathed right before he took my mouth with his in a kiss that was more incendiary than the hottest flame. I knew it would burn; I only hoped I could withstand the pain he'd inevitably cause me.

Everyone knew Dutch Miller was already in love, and it wasn't with me.

About the Author

I gave myself the gift of writing a book for my birthday one year. A few short years and thirty-plus books later, I've hit a couple of best-seller lists and have had the time of my life. The joy for me is in writing them, but nothing makes me happier than hearing from a reader who tells me I've made her laugh or cry or gasp or hold her breath or stay up all night because she can't put my book down.

The women I write are self-confident, strong, with wills of their own, and hearts as big as the Colorado sky. The men are sublimely sexy, seductive alphas who rise to the challenge of capturing the sweet soul of a woman whose heart they'll hold in the palm of their hand forever. Add in a couple of neck-snapping twists and turns, a page-turning mystery, and a swoon-worthy HEA, and you'll be holding one of my books in your hands.

I love to hear from my readers. You can contact me at heather@heatherslade.com

To keep up with my latest news and releases, please visit my website at www.heatherslade.com to sign up for my newsletter.

MORE FROM AUTHOR HEATHER SLADE

BUTLER RANCH
Prequel: *Kade's Worth*
Book One: *Brodie*
Book Two: *Maddox*
Book Three: *Naughton*
Book Four: *Mercer*
Book Five: *Kade*

K19 SECURITY SOLUTIONS
Book One: *Razor*
Book Two: *Gunner*
Book Three: *Mistletoe*
Book Four: *Mantis*
Book Five: *Dutch*
Book Six: *Striker*
Book Seven: *Monk*
Book Eight: *Halo*
Book Nine: *Tackle*
Coming soon:
Book Ten: *Onyx*

MILITARY INTELLIGENCE
SECTION 6
Book One: *Shiver*
Book Two: *Wilder*
Book Three: *Pinch*
Book Four: *Shadow*

THE INVINCIBLES
Book One: *Decked*
Book Two: *Edged*
Book Three: *Grinded*
Book Four: *Riled*
Book Five: *Smoked*
Book Six: *Bucked*
Book Seven: *Irished*
Coming soon:
Book Eight: *Sainted*

ROARING FORK RANCH
Coming soon:
Book One: *Roughstock*
Book Two: *Rockstar*

COWBOYS OF
CRESTED BUTTE
Book One: *Fall for Me*
Book Two: *Dance with Me*
Book Three: *Kiss Me Cowboy*
Book Four: *Stay with Me*
Book Five: *Win Me Over*

COCKY HERO CLUB
Undercover Agent

KB WORLDS
EVERYDAY HEROES:
Handled

Made in the USA
Columbia, SC
09 June 2021